“Mac, … declare a truce.

Maggie kept her voice light. “I don’t know what it is about you—about us—that always makes me overreact.”

Mac grinned at her. “I’ve noticed that your emotions do run a bit high. Seems like every time we’ve been together, I’ve had to beat a hasty retreat. Not a very satisfactory state of affairs for a military man.”

“Well, what about that truce?”

“Nope. No truce. A truce implies both parties shake hands, retire from the field of honor and go their separate ways.”

“A cease-fire, then? An end to hostilities?”

“Not good enough. Nothing so imprecise for us.”

“Well, for heaven’s sake, what *do* you want?” Maggie asked, exasperated.

“I won’t settle for anything less than unconditional surrender!”

Merline Lovelace was, until recently, a career air force officer who served tours of duty in Vietnam, at the Pentagon and at bases all over the world. During her years in uniform, she met and married her own handsome colonel—and stored up enough exciting adventures to keep her fingers flying over the keyboard for years to come.

Merline's new career as a writer is off to a great start. In addition to writing *Maggie and Her Colonel* for Worldwide's Stolen Moments line, she's proud to announce her first three Harlequin Historical romances. Scheduled for release in May 1994 is *Alena,* followed by *Sweet Song of Love* in July and *Phaedra* in September. Not only that, her first novel in the Silhouette Desire series will be published in August.

To my dad, Merl,
who gave me his name,
a childhood filled with love
and a hopeless addiction to golf.

MAGGIE AND HER COLONEL

Merline Lovelace

TORONTO • NEW YORK • LONDON
AMSTERDAM • PARIS • SYDNEY • HAMBURG
STOCKHOLM • ATHENS • TOKYO • MILAN
MADRID • WARSAW • BUDAPEST • AUCKLAND

Special thanks and acknowledgment to
Merline Lovelace

ISBN 0-373-83273-7

MAGGIE AND HER COLONEL

This edition published by arrangement with Harlequin Enterprises B. V.

Printed in U.S.A.

Chapter One

"Just who the hell is this Dr. Wescott, and where does he get off disapproving my test?"

Seated in the outer reception area, Maggie heard every angry word. She shook her head and shared a wry grin with the secretary perched behind a large modular desk unit. The older woman winked, then turned to listen with unabashed interest to the exchange taking place in the commander's office.

"Dr. Wescott is our new chief of Environmental Engineering and is waiting outside to discuss the issue with you when you calm down, Mac."

Her boss's measured tones provided a sharp contrast to the visitor's deep angry growl.

"I'm as calm as I'm likely to get over this. Bring him in."

The secretary answered the intercom on its first short ring. Gray curls bouncing, she nodded toward the open door.

Here we go, Maggie thought. She squared her shoulders to take full advantage of her considerable height and entered the inner office. She could tell from the glint in her boss's eyes that he was thoroughly enjoying the situation, the old reprobate.

"Colonel MacRae, this is Dr. Wescott. She joined our staff a week ago. One of her first projects was your proposed test."

Maggie had to admire the visitor's composure, even if she *had* decided to dislike him on principle. MacRae's blue eyes narrowed dangerously for a moment when she entered, and he slanted a sharp glance at Maggie's grinning supervisor. He showed no other signs of surprise that Dr. Wescott was not the man he expected, however, and took her hand in a firm grip.

Maggie felt a strange sensation as she looked up, and up, into the man's eyes. He was a linebacker in a blue air force uniform, for heaven's sake. She couldn't remember the last time she felt dwarfed by any man. At five foot eight in her stocking feet, she was usually at least eye level with her co-workers and acquaintances.

"Dr. Wescott, Colonel MacRae is commander of the armament division of Wright Laboratory here on base. He's concerned that you disapproved the propulsion test his lab wants to conduct and would like to discuss the project with you personally."

With that bland introduction, Ed Stockton sat back to enjoy the fireworks. He'd only worked with the young woman who now headed his Environmental Engineering department for a week, but he'd put his money on her, hands down. She'd made mincemeat of one of the other department heads who'd mistaken her blond good looks and laughing green eyes for those of a professional lightweight. The lady knew her stuff and didn't take any nonsense from anyone.

MacRae started his attack even as they moved to the conference table.

"Since you're new here, Dr. Wescott, you may not fully understand the implications of this test for Eglin Air Force Base and for the lab. It involves over a million dollars in reimbursable costs and is vital to the space program."

The hairs on Maggie's neck bristled. She could almost forgive this man for the unconscious chauvinism she'd overheard while she sat in the reception room. Most men, and women, of her acquaintance assumed engineers were of the male persuasion. But no one questioned her professional competence and lived to tell about it. Inwardly seething, she kept her voice level.

"Colonel, I fully appreciate the implications of this test for Eglin. The chemical you want to use as a propellant is highly volatile and has never been tested anywhere in the quantity you propose. Your people have done a poor job in addressing potential impacts in their environmental assessment."

Maggie seated herself at the conference table and laid the folder with her notes aside. She'd done some quick reading since the call had come to report to her boss's office. She had her facts down cold.

"The U.S. Fish and Wildlife Service has already issued a statement of concern over your test's threat to endangered species. Even if I wanted to override their objections, which I don't, Eglin would be slapped with a notice of violation. Not only would the Wildlife folks have scrubbed this test, but they might hold all our other tests hostage while we negotiated with them. This base is too important a test facility to the Department of Defense to allow a poorly planned, inadequately researched project like this to close it down, even temporarily."

Mac MacRae leveled a hard stare at the young woman across the conference table. She must have ordered her Ph.D. through the mail, he thought. With her mass of golden curls that tumbled wildly over her shoulders, she looked about eighteen. Only when he noticed the fine lines fanning out from the corners of her eyes did he revise his estimate of her age, if not her capabilities. Maybe she was old enough, but surely not experienced enough to make the kind of judgment she had.

His lips settled into a grim line, and he gave her his full attention. By the time she was halfway through her succinct review of the situation, he'd stopped seeing her curly hair and sensuous lips. Instead, he focused on clear green eyes that looked at him with distinct challenge and more than a hint of disapproval. He listened in silence, then sat back in his chair to consider the facts she'd laid before him.

Maggie refused to let MacRae's silence disconcert her. She held his gaze steadily and used the pause to take a mental inventory of the man facing her. Those penetrating blue eyes seemed out of place in a tanned face with a nose that looked like someone had taken a fist to it more than once. Or a shoulder, Maggie thought, in keeping with his linebacker appearance. She noted with some satisfaction the silver that liberally laced his dark hair. He wasn't as young as he looked at first glance, she thought, unknowingly mirroring MacRae's assessment of her. Although why that thought should give her satisfaction, she had no idea. She was so absorbed in her private review that she jumped at the deep gravelly voice.

"I apologize, Dr. Wescott. You've obviously put more effort into studying this project than I realized. I'll have my people redefine the test parameters. I'd appreciate it if you'd work with us closely so we can modify the test to satisfy all environmental concerns."

His response surprised Maggie. She'd had her hackles up and was ready for a long argument. Hard experience had taught her that some men were congenitally unable to give in gracefully to a woman. She would've bet her last dollar this hulking male was one of them. His reasonableness left her feeling slightly deflated.

Before she could frame a coherent reply, MacRae got to his feet and shook Ed Stockton's hand. He turned to take Maggie's hand again, and her pulse seemed to jump at the hard warmth that enveloped her palm. She was sure she only imagined that he held her hand longer than he had the first time. Tugging her fingers loose as nonchalantly as possible, Maggie used the excuse of gathering up her papers to put some distance between them. For some reason, this man disturbed her. Maybe it was his size. He was a veritable mountain, for heaven's sake. By the time she'd stuffed the report haphazardly into a file, he was gone.

"Just who was that masked man?" she asked her boss.

Ed Stockton laughed at her rueful grimace. "I've known MacRae a long time, Maggie. There isn't a more brilliant physicist or better commander in the air force."

"He looks more like a football player than a scientist," Maggie commented.

"You aren't exactly the stereotype Ph.D., either," Ed responded blandly. "Actually I think Mac did play football at the Air Force Academy. Now he's a test pilot, but one of the weird ones. He actually finds the science of what makes those tubes of steel fly more fascinating than the flying itself. He's brilliant, but when he has a hot project in the works, he's like a bulldog. The man's made my life miserable more times than I can count with his demands for range support for his propulsion tests. It did the old heart good to see him put in his place for once."

Maggie knew her boss well enough by now not to take him seriously. A senior colonel, Ed Stockton could give as good as he got and then some. His gruff voice hid a sharp precise mind and a total dedication to the air force. He needed both to command the nine-hundred-plus civil engineers, military and civilian, who were responsible for maintaining Eglin Air Force Base. The largest air base in the world, Eglin covered a land area of more than half a million acres and ate up most of the western half of Florida's panhandle. It boasted thousands of miles of roads and hundreds of buildings and test facilities.

Maggie was just beginning to appreciate the vast size of the base, as well as the scope of her job. As chief of Environmental Engineering, her responsibilities included anything and everything that might have an impact on the environment on that half-million acres. When she'd first arrived, she'd outlined a schedule to visit every hazardous-material site, fuel-storage area and restricted-test area on base. It would take her six months to cover them all.

Maggie had responded on impulse to the ad for an environmental engineer at Eglin. She'd worked for the government before on some classified projects in Washington and knew enough about the test business to win an immediate job interview. Unlikely as it seemed at first to either of them, she and Ed Stockton had hit it off from the first few minutes of the interview.

Maggie knew that her extensive credentials and her high-powered industry job she gave up to come to Florida had impressed Stockton. He'd asked her why she wanted to come to "redneck country," as he put, after working at corporate level for a major oil conglomerate in Houston. She'd responded that she needed a change and wanted to get back to field-level work. At Stockton's quizzical look, she added gently that she had personal reasons, as well, which were none of his business.

Maggie considered her private life her own affair. If the crusty colonel interviewing her wasn't satisfied with her professional credentials, she knew there were plenty of others who would be. Stockton was more than happy—with both her credentials and her feisty spirit, so like his own. He'd hired her on the spot and had enjoyed the reactions of the conservative local populace ever since she'd arrived. Just as he'd enjoyed MacRae's narrow-eyed appraisal of her. Ed leaned back in his swivel chair and regarded his newest employee.

"Work with MacRae on this test, Maggie. He's right about its importance. If there's a way to do it safely, let's find it."

"I'll give it my best, Ed, although I doubt I'll have much to do with the big man himself. He'll probably assign the task of convincing me to some lowly engineer."

"Possibly," Ed agreed. "Just don't be surprised if you find him taking a personal interest in this project. It's a big one."

Chapter Two

Maggie's next encounter with "the mountain," as she'd privately dubbed him, came sooner than either she or Ed Stockton had imagined. She ran into him, literally, the next evening.

She'd been invited by the chief of Natural Resources to join a nighttime expedition to one of the base's protected beaches. Natural Resources was responsible for wildlife and timber management on the sprawling Eglin complex. The chief of that division went about his work with a contagious enthusiasm. With Ed Stockton's support, he'd enlisted a local school to help with the annual turtle-hatching. Maggie listened with smiling skepticism as he explained how she could help.

"Really, Maggie, half the squadron turns out, as much to help supervise the kids as work the turtles. Most of the fun is watching the youngsters see nature at work."

"Come on, Pete, don't the folks in this corner of Florida have anything better to do on Friday night? Do you really expect me to believe you've got several hundred adults and as many kids coming out to watch turtles hatch?"

Pete smiled through his bushy beard. Now here was a man who fit his biologist image, Maggie thought. Unlike a certain hulking scientist.

"Not just watch," Pete protested. "We have to work them. The loggerhead sea turtles are one of the endangered species that are protected by law. But mama loggerhead isn't a very responsible parent, and that makes our job difficult. She deposits her eggs on Eglin's beaches, then swims off into the gulf. My people have spent the past few months building wire cages to protect the nests from predators."

Pete's earnestness won Maggie's interest, and she leaned forward to peer over his shoulder at the map showing the various nesting sites.

"The eggs are just now starting to hatch. Unfortunately, on cloudy nights like tonight, the baby turtles can't see the moon's reflection on water to guide them to the sea. They get disoriented, lose their way and die."

"I would think a couple of hundred inquisitive schoolkids would only add to the poor baby turtles' confusion," Maggie joked.

"Come out to Site 15 tonight with me and see. Trust me," Pete said, placing a hairy paw on his plaid-covered chest. "It'll be one of the adventures of your life."

Later that night, as the moon darted in and out of dark clouds, Maggie stood a short distance apart from a milling group of adults and preteens that Pete was organizing. She'd driven out with him and listened to his detailed explanation of the night's activities, but still felt a bit foolish among a bunch of strangers baby-sitting turtles of all things. She shivered slightly in her lightweight jacket. So much for balmy Florida nights and swaying palm trees, she thought.

Even the cool May night air, however, couldn't dampen her natural ebullience for long. She stood on a slight rise and caught her breath as the moon peeked around the edge of a cloud, bathing the beach with soft light. White sand, undulating dunes and the iridescent ripple of the waves washing in combined to make a magical seascape. Maggie drank in the serene beauty of the night, disturbed only by the excited noise of a dozen children trying to be quiet.

She turned toward the nest area, noticing that the kids had formed a line from the dunes to the shore. When they switched on their flashlights, a wave of high-pitched giggles and muted adult exclamations drifted across the night air. Despite herself, Maggie felt a thrill as she saw hundreds of tiny dark forms begin to make their squiggly way to the sea. She started to run down to join the line, but crashed headlong into a very large dark form coming from the side.

Hard hands gripped one arm and one breast, trying to keep her from falling. The hand on her breast shifted almost immediately to her other arm, but not before Maggie's startled glance had looked up, way up, into equally startled eyes.

Maggie's ready sense of humor overcame her momentary embarrassment. "I know you wanted us to work closely, Colonel, but isn't this above and beyond the call of duty?"

"Dr. Wescott, I'd have recognized you anywhere."

At Maggie's indignant gasp, MacRae added, "From the moonlight glinting on that wild head of hair."

His wicked smile told Maggie that he knew very well she'd thought he was referring to his quick but very thorough exploration of her breast. The thought of his hand on it brought an unexpected tingle to the very area he had pressed so briefly. She stepped back quickly out of his hold.

"What are you doing here, Colonel? Scouting out the next site to blow up with one of your super ray guns?"

Mac smiled down at her. "You've been listening to that old goat Stockton too much. I don't blow up every part of his precious range. Only the selected portions he grudgingly allows the rest of us to use. Actually I'm here in my other official capacity tonight. Those are my two boys over there, trying not to stomp too many turtles to death as they help 'save' them."

He waved in the general direction of the line of children. Maggie saw a couple of flashlights dance wildly in response. Even in the darkness, she guessed, his kids could pick out their giant of a father. She firmly suppressed a surprising twinge of disappointment at the thought of his having children. Of course he had kids, and he probably had a dainty demure little wife, as well. Maggie took a step away from him.

"I better get over there and help, too, or I'll lose my environmentalist badge."

Mac fell in beside her as she headed toward the line. Inexplicably, some of the adventure of the night had dimmed for Maggie.

"Dad, Dad, can me and Danny spend the night at Joey's?"

A sand-covered shadow ran full tilt toward them out of the darkness. Maggie barely avoided her second collision of the night, but Mac wasn't as lucky. He caught the youngster, who appeared to be about nine, under his arms and swirled him around in a shower of sand, wet jeans and giggles.

"Mind your manners, Davey. Say hello to Dr. Wescott. She works at the base, too."

Davey extended a damp sandy hand to Maggie. His grin, as he introduced himself, was a miniature duplicate of one she had seen smiling down at her just a few moments ago. Heavens, there were three of these males loose on society!

"Please, Dad. Joey's mom promised to make fudge tonight. Can we go?"

"Let me talk to her first, son, and make sure it's all right."

As the child dashed back to his place in line, Mac excused himself. "I need to catch Joey's mom before they overwhelm her. I'm not sure she knows what she's getting into with those twins of mine. They've been through half a dozen full-time housekeepers in the past few years. The latest has worked out only because she used to be a warden in a woman's prison."

He started to walk away, then turned back. "What the heck's your first name, anyway? I feel like we've passed the Dr. Wescott stage."

"I'll tell you, if you'll tell me what goes in front of the 'Mac' in MacRae."

For the first time, Maggie saw the big man slightly discomposed.

"It's Alastair, after my Scottish grandfather. Most of the folks who know me have managed to forget that. Mac'll do just fine. Your turn."

"Maggie, short for Marguerite. After my French grandmother."

He left Maggie with a smile. She wandered toward the line, thinking of their brief conversation. After their initial meeting, Maggie never would have imagined enjoying herself with the incredible hunk so much. She had just reached the point of wondering about the string of housekeepers when he was back.

"All clear. The boys are set, and I have an unexpected free evening. Do you want to go hatch turtles with me?"

The moon came out from behind a scudding cloud, lighting the beach and Maggie's night. She resisted an almost overwhelming urge to put her hand in the one he was holding out to her.

"Wouldn't Mrs. Colonel MacRae mind you going off to hatch turtles with another woman?"

Maggie was nothing if not direct. She had learned to be to succeed in a field still dominated by men.

Mac was equally direct. "My wife died in a car crash six years ago. It's just the boys and me." He looked out at the sea briefly, then deliberately lightened the somber mood. "Danny and Davey have been trying to marry me off for years to any woman who can cook. You don't have a diploma from a gourmet-cooking school tucked away with all your other degrees, do you?"

"Nope, you're safe."

"Good, come on, then. There's another nest a little way down the beach, minus kids. Pete told me about it. Incidentally he mentioned that he'd be here late. I told him I'd take you home if you want to leave before he does."

Maggie stared at him in wry amusement. The man sure moved fast for someone his size.

They spent the next hour alternately escorting hatchlings to the sea and sitting next to a small fire set in the protection of the dunes. Mac provided a thermos of hot coffee laced with rum. Obviously he'd done turtle duty before.

She found the man beside her fascinating. He laughed and joked easily with the other members of the small group. In between dashes to the sea, he kept Maggie amused with a light running commentary on the joys of parenting twin boys.

For his part, Mac couldn't keep his eyes off her mobile expressive face with those green eyes gleaming in the moonlight. Nor off her long legs and the firm tush outlined to perfection by her tight jeans. She had a light and laughing personality that attracted Mac even more than her trim figure. When the last hatchlings finally made their way to the surf, he took Maggie's arm and led her away from the small fire toward a Jeep parked at the edge of the dunes.

"Mac, I'm cold," Maggie protested, looking back longingly at the fire and the thermos of doctored coffee Mac had left with the remaining group.

"Me, too. We'll get warm in the car. My jeans are wet clear up to my thighs."

"That's a lot of wet," Maggie said, her voice solemn.

He grinned and helped her into the Jeep. Joining her, he turned on the ignition and the heater. Welcome warmth began to fill the cab, along with the soft strains of a country-and-western ballad from the radio.

"Better?" he asked.

"Mmm, much."

Maggie propped her knees up against the dash and leaned back in the seat, drinking in the sight of shadowed moonlight dancing on the sea and her tingling awareness of the man beside her. Idly she wondered if she'd have a chance to see Mac again once she started working with his people on the test project. She certainly hoped so.

Mac's low voice cut through the stillness. "I was impressed with your grasp of the issues on our propulsion test. For someone so new to the base, you've certainly picked up on our business quickly."

"I may be new to Eglin, but I'm not new to testing," she told him. "I worked in Research and Development on the Air Staff for a while before I moved to private industry."

"What made you come back to defense work?"

Maggie found that Mac's presence was proving to be a major distraction. That, and the way his arm stretched across the back of the seat. She had to think a couple of moments before she could come up with a response.

"It was time for a change," she finally managed.

"I'm glad," he said, and smiled.

At her inquiring look, his hand slid off the seat back and burrowed under the weight of her hair. It settled on her nape, and Maggie felt the tender rasp of his callused fingertips all the way down to her toes.

"I'm glad you needed a change, Maggie. I'm glad you're here."

Maggie swallowed and looked up to see his eyes glinting silvery blue in the moonlight.

"Me, too, Mac," she whispered.

With a lopsided grin, he moved his arm down to wrap it around her waist. His muscles barely shifted as he lifted her easily across the gearshift and into his lap. She half-sat, half-lay across his iron-hard thighs.

"I've been wanting to do this since turtle number twenty-seven," he murmured.

His dark head bent toward her, and Maggie felt his lips close over hers. He tasted of coffee and rum and delicious male. Letting her eyes drift closed, she savored the slow languorous way his lips moved over hers.

She smiled up at him when he pulled back moments later. "Why did you wait so long?"

Mac gave a little groan. The hand around her waist tightened as he fit her more fully against his chest, and her head angled back for his kiss. When she moaned softly in an unconscious echo, his tongue delved in to explore her mouth. Maggie's last rational thought was that she hadn't necked in a parked car since junior high. She hadn't realized what she was missing.

A long time later they surfaced. Mac tilted her chin up so he could see her face in the moonlight. With a grunt of pure male satisfaction he took in her half-closed dreamy eyes and swollen lips.

"Lord, you look great in the moonlight, woman. Especially with that hair of yours glinting that way."

When she only smiled in response, Mac ran his finger gently back and forth across her lower lip. Maggie had thought the feel of his lips on hers erotic. This finger business was about to drive her crazy. Instinctively she opened her mouth and captured his finger in a teasing nip.

"You little cat."

Mac bent her back over his arm as far as the truck door would allow and kissed her again. His hand started to move toward the zipper on her jacket, then stopped a tantalizing few inches away from her breast.

Dragging in a harsh breath, he lifted his head and dropped his hand to rest on the curve of her hip. "Lord, I'm sorry, Maggie."

She blinked. "Sorry?"

"I'm acting like some pimply teenager on his first date. I must be crazy, trying to grope you in the front seat of a car."

Flustered, Maggie stared up at him. She wasn't about to admit that she wanted to be groped, front seat or back. That she hadn't been kissed like that by anyone, pimply or otherwise, in this lifetime. That her nipples had tingled in anticipation as his hand started to open her jacket. She swallowed and tried to take in his next words.

"I can't believe I lost control to the point where I was ready to do something I'd wallop the boys for in a few years. Would it help any if I said you and the moonlight are a fatal combination and I couldn't help myself?"

A slow wave of embarrassment washed over Maggie as she listened to his apology. Here she was, a grown woman with a string of degrees, trading kisses with a man she hardly knew. In a Jeep, no less. Obviously, Mac hadn't expected her uninhibited response—any more than she had herself.

She shifted off his lap and scrambled awkwardly to her seat.

"I'd like to go home now."

"Maggie—"

"Now, please." Thoroughly mortified, and a little hurt by his rejection, Maggie stared straight ahead.

Mac studied her stony profile and cursed himself for being such a clumsy idiot. It wasn't as if he was totally out of practice. He hadn't been celibate all these years since Anne's death, but normally he managed a bit more finesse. He didn't know what it was about this woman now staring at the sea that started his hormones raging. Since his first meeting with her, he'd felt far more than a professional interest. That interest had ripened to a deep attraction as he'd watched her sparkle in the firelight and shimmer in the moonlight.

He'd responded to her looks as any healthy male would, but it was more than that. She'd put him calmly and efficiently in his place in Stockton's office. Instead of turning him off, he found himself intrigued by the brain behind the face. By the whole woman. When she careened into him tonight and he felt her firm breast in his hand, Mac had decided instantly to follow up on that promising lead. He just hadn't planned to let it go quite so far, so soon.

"Look at me, Maggie. Please."

He waited until she speared him with a cold challenging look. "I'm sorry. I didn't mean to come on to you like some sex-starved jerk. We're going to be working together closely for the next few weeks. I don't want you to be... uncomfortable around me."

Mac could have kicked himself as soon as the words were out. They sounded pompous and all wrong, and he could see that was just the way Maggie heard them. Anger quickly replaced the stony stillness on her face.

"Look, Colonel, I've never yet let private feelings interfere with my professional dealings, and you aren't the man to change that. If you're through beating your breast over this evening's fiasco, would you please take me home? Or shall I find another ride?"

Mac muttered a curse under his breath. Obviously he couldn't recover tonight. However, he hadn't risen to the top of his profession without learning his trade. Any good military man knew when to beat a strategic retreat and marshal his forces for another day. Without another word he drove the Jeep out of the tall dunes and onto the highway.

During the ride home Maggie stoked her simmering anger at the man seated next to her. So he was a world-class hunk who looked as good in his uniform as in the worn jeans he was wearing tonight. So he had a slow easy smile that crinkled his eyes. So some people thought he was brilliant. She knew better. The man was a jerk, just as he himself said, and the less she dealt with him the better. The fact that he'd stopped kissing her when she was warm and willing had nothing at all to do with the matter. At least that's what she finally managed to convince herself of by the time she'd soaked in a hot tub and buried her head under a mound of covers.

Chapter Three

Maggie wasn't sure whether it was the insistent ringing of the doorbell or the loud barking that woke her the next morning. She poked her head out from under the tangled covers, pushed a pile of hair out of her eyes and squinted at the clock.

It was only seven-thirty, for heaven's sake! And a Saturday morning, as best she could recall. What idiot was making such a racket so early? It took another few moments for the fact to penetrate that the ringing doorbell was hers and the barking didn't seem to be going away.

Muttering something that wouldn't have done much for her professional image, Maggie climbed out of bed. She searched among the jumble in her closet for a robe. She hadn't had time in the week she'd been here to unpack, but household chores were pretty low in her list of priorities. By the time she'd found a short beach robe to cover her nightshirt, the doorbell had begun to grate on her nerves, and she was seriously considering changing her opinion on animal euthanasia.

Her sleepy irritation changed to surprise when she opened the door of her rented condo. Three pairs of male eyes surveyed her. Four, if the huge creature who treated her to one more ear-splitting bark before plopping down on her doorstep happened to be a him.

"Mornin', ma'am." Mac's blue eyes twinkled down at her confusion. "I just collected the boys from Joey's house, and they swear three pounds of fudge barely kept them from starving to death last night. We're on our way to our favorite restaurant for breakfast. Since you're new in town, we thought you might like to join us for some local down-home cooking."

In answer to her skeptical look, one of the boys chimed in. "Honest, ma'am. Felix makes the best grits in town. Probably in all of Florida. Maybe in the world." Another enthusiastic bark seconded the boy's earnest opinion.

Maggie smiled down at him, then gave Mac an inquiring glance.

"This is Daniel." Mac ruffled one dark head affectionately. "You met David last night. They're otherwise known as the Terrible Twosome or, more politely, the Scourges of Northwest Florida."

"Aw, come on, Dad." Davey grinned up at him. "We're not that bad, at least not all the time."

Maggie suddenly realized that her front doorstep was not exactly the proper place to be standing in a short robe and carrying on an extended conversation. Not that she should be carrying on a conversation with these three males in a short robe at all. Correction, make that four males, Maggie amended as the big hairy beast sniffed a ceramic pot gracing her doorstep, then lifted his leg to drown her poor potted mums. Thank goodness they were artificial, Maggie thought. Gardening was another domestic task she had little interest in or talent for.

"Woof—bad boy!" three male voices chastised the dog in unison. The dog drooped his head in a semblance of repentance for a few seconds. Then a squirrel in the yard caught his attention and he bounded off.

"Woof, come back!" Davey yelled.

"Interesting name," Maggie said as the dog returned, tail wagging. She stood aside. "Why don't the bunch of you come in for a moment while I put on something more presentable?"

Mac's eyes told her that he found her eminently presentable, but he prudently kept silent as she led them into a light airy living room.

Maggie had fallen in love with this condo the first moment she'd seen it. Since it fronted the emerald-green waters of the Gulf of Mexico, the rent was high. She considered the spacious rooms well worth the price, though. At least they had seemed spacious until her three—four—unexpected guests filled them.

Mac caught her arm as she turned for the hallway. "Please come, Maggie," he said softly. "I at least owe you breakfast for last night."

"You don't owe me anything at all," she began, only to stop abruptly as she noted two pairs of very interested blue eyes fixed on her and Mac.

"What happened last night, Dad? Did you put the make on Dr. Westly?"

Out of the mouths of babes, Maggie thought. She folded her arms and turned to watch how Mac handled this one. He got himself in. Let him get himself out.

"It's Dr. Wescott, Davey. And I guess I did come on a bit strong with her. Breakfast is my way of apology."

Maggie had to admire MacRae's honesty with his sons, even if she didn't particularly like being the subject of it. She gave a silent groan as the boys turned their bright inquisitive eyes back to her. She forestalled the highly personal questions hovering on their lips.

"Apology accepted. And it's Maggie, guys. Give me a few minutes to get dressed, and I'll take you up on your offer of grits."

"That's great, Maggie. But don't take too long, okay? You won't mess with all that female stuff, will you?" Davey, or maybe it was Danny, managed to project a superb impression of imminent starvation.

"I wonder where they picked up that little bit of sexism," Maggie tossed at Mac as she moved past him.

Five minutes later she was back, dressed in snug jeans and a soft red sweater. Her only concession to "female" stuff was a red band that caught her long curls up in a wispy concoction Mac found utterly enticing.

He forced himself to repress the mental urge to pull that band slowly back out of her hair and watch the tawny mass spill across his arm. *Come on, man,* he told himself, *you're here to make amends, not make matters worse.* With that admonishment, he shepherded Maggie and his tribe out of the apartment and into his Jeep.

Maggie found herself amazed at the variety and scope of interest displayed by the two lively nine-year-olds. During the short ride their conversation ranged from the fate of the turtles hatched last night to hockey strategy to some strange rock group whose name seemed to be composed mostly of dead things. She sat back, content to enjoy their company and let the crisp Florida air fan her hunger.

An hour later the boys watched with open admiration as she pushed back her second empty grits bowl. It joined the litter of empty biscuit platters and gravy boats on the table.

"Gimme a break, guys," Maggie said, noting their expressions. "I'm a big girl. I need a lot of sustenance."

The boys and their father flashed identical grins. Maggie felt her heart thump against her full stomach. It must be heartburn from all this food, she thought. She couldn't be falling for three bothersome males who wouldn't even let a gal sleep late on Saturday mornings.

She sipped her coffee, feeling full and strangely happy in the midst of the noisy clatter of the restaurant. When she met Mac's look, he let loose with one of those slow easy smiles that started at the corners of his mouth and ended up lightening his blue eyes to silvery gray. It almost made Maggie forget where she was.

"Forgiven?" he mouthed at her over the boy's heads. She smiled back and gave a slow nod.

"At the risk of overwhelming you with MacRaes, would you like to fill the next couple of hours with fresh air, terrifying suspense and unmitigated violence? The boys have soccer practice in half an hour. They always perform better before admiring females."

"Daaad," the twins chorused, but they turned identical hopeful looks on Maggie.

Maggie rubbed her full tummy as if in deep thought. "I guess I need to do something to repay the guys for the best grits I've ever had. Sure, I can cheer them on for an hour or so."

Mac's thigh rubbed against Maggie's jean-clad leg as they sat on the hard bleachers. She found his taut muscles much more fascinating than the controlled mayhem that passed for kids' soccer. She retained barely enough consciousness of the game to return the twins' waves after each spectacular play, which, given the wild charges up and down the field, didn't happen too often. The bleachers were crowded with noisy parents, all no doubt hoping their offspring would work off some energy. Maggie noticed the speculative glances other parents had given Mac when he arrived with boys, dog and herself in tow.

Mac had returned several friendly greetings, but didn't linger beyond brief introductions. He wanted some time alone with the tawny-haired creature next to him—if you could consider being surrounded by yelling soccer parents on a crowded bleacher alone, he thought with a wry grimace. Actually the strategy worked better than he'd anticipated. From long years of practice he caught all the boy's more energetic moves while he kept his attention and gaze mostly on the woman beside him. She fascinated him more by the minute.

"We all appreciated not being kept waiting for 'female stuff' this morning," he told her, gazing down at her fresh glowing complexion. "The boys, because they were about to expire with hunger on the spot. Me, because I find you look even better in the light of day than in the moonlight."

"I'm not sure you ought to bring up the subject of moonlight. I'm still trying to sort last night out."

Mac winced at her directness. She leaned her elbows back against the seat behind them and studied him from under thick gold-tipped lashes. "You confused me," she added. "My own response to you confused me."

"Well, confusion is better than the disgusted looks I was getting last night." He grinned down at her, unrepentant. "Our housekeeper gets back tomorrow afternoon, Maggie. Would you have dinner with me tomorrow night? Just us, I promise. No boys or turtles or dogs."

Maggie gave him a long considering look. She should say no. Things were moving too fast with this man. He overwhelmed her, both physically and with his exuberant family. Besides, there was the project to consider. They might find themselves on opposite sides of a very nasty debate before too long. Despite all that, Maggie found herself nodding.

"Yes," she got out, right before an errant soccer ball rocketed toward their heads and they both ducked, laughing.

Chapter Four

After the game Maggie spent the rest of Saturday and most of Sunday at her cubbyhole of an office. She might hold a Phi Beta Kappa key from MIT and have a good ten years' experience in environmental issues, but the complexity of Eglin's operations awed her. Like any professional, she wanted to learn as much as she could as quickly as possible.

Late Sunday afternoon she found the folder on the laboratory test under a stack of files. Although she felt comfortable with her initial assessment, she decided to go through the documentation again. Her growing personal interest in the man behind the test had nothing to do with it, she told herself. This was business.

The new chemical proposed as a propellant could make a major difference in the Department of Defense space program. Although highly volatile, it was inexpensive to formulate and readily available. Maggie had read a lot about it, had even been involved in another minor experiment involving it a few years ago. But this test represented a major milestone in its practical application. She spent a good hour rereading the report and doing her own analysis of the test parameters.

She sat back in her chair, brow furrowed and doubts still unresolved. The propellant was incredibly dangerous, more so than most of the exotic explosives and chemicals tested at Eglin. Maggie knew commercial concerns were just beginning to consider it as a possible source of power, but no one had figured out how to reduce its volatility to safe levels yet.

As she reviewed possible test impacts, Maggie began to appreciate just why Eglin Air Force Base covered an area larger than a small state. The test business involved a lot of unknowns—dropping bombs or firing missiles for the first time and recording their properties. The fliers and engineers required a large safety footprint for their tests. Unfortunately the footprint included habitats of several endangered species, highways that had to be closed during tests and encroaching civilian communities. All of them had to be considered in the environmental analysis for each major new test. Mac's staff hadn't adequately addressed all the environmental impacts if this propellant lived up to its dangerous potential.

She made a few hasty notes and stuffed the folder into her tote to take home with her for yet another look. She put the other folders back in her drawer and glanced at the wall clock. She wanted plenty of time to prepare for her dinner date this evening with her enigmatic colonel.

If Mac's soft whistle when she opened her door to him later was any indication, her preparation time had been well spent. She felt the impact of his glinting approval from her hair, held up with combs on top of her head, down the length of the shimmery green silk pantsuit to her high-heeled sandals.

"I'm not exactly sure how anyone encased in cloth from neck to toe can manage to look mostly undressed, but you come close."

"I think I'll take that as a compliment," Maggie said, moving aside to let him in. "Wearing outrageous clothes is one of the few advantages a tall woman has in life over the dainty types."

Maggie smiled to herself as she turned to shut the door. She'd bought the outfit because of the way the silk clung sensuously to every curve. She didn't have that many of them, and if this little outfit helped Mac notice the few she had, it was worth every penny.

Mac would have disagreed with her assessment of her attractions had he known it. His eyes roamed appreciatively from her slender hips to her small high breasts. The jade-green tunic outlined them clearly, hinting at the nubs in their centers before falling in graceful folds. Surveying the way the fabric moved as Maggie did, Mac's feelings underwent a subtle change. From masculine appreciation, he began to experience a possessive desire to keep Maggie's curves to himself. He felt a surprisingly primitive urge to wrap her in a shapeless blanket so that only he knew what was beneath.

Unaware of his thoughts, Maggie turned to pick up her small gold purse. Mac barely stifled a groan when the silk outlined the delicious curves of her derriere as she leaned down. It was with a somewhat grim expression that he escorted Maggie to his car.

He managed to relax over dinner. The sight of Maggie demolishing a grilled red snapper, a generous portion of steamed rice and half a loaf of crusty French bread, along with a bottle of perfectly chilled chardonnay, restored his balance.

Maggie sighed as she leaned back in her chair. "That was heaven."

"It's nice to share a meal with someone who appreciates it," he responded, lifting his wineglass in her direction.

"Which is a very tactful way of saying I eat too much." Maggie laughed. "I guess being tall has another advantage, besides allowing me to wear outrageous clothes. It takes a lot more to fill me up. And I can enjoy every morsel." She grinned unrepentantly over the rim of her wineglass.

"Yes, and I can think of at least one more advantage." At her inquiring look, he stood and held out his hand. "I've been looking forward to dancing with someone whose nose won't tickle my belly-button. Come dance with me, Maggie m'girl."

Mac decided he liked the feel of the woman in his arms. Very much. She fitted him perfectly. Ignoring the glances other men in the room directed at Maggie, he enjoyed the feel of her warm flesh through the smooth material as he moved his hand slowly up and down her back. To distract himself from what he could feel at her front, he nuzzled a soft tendril of hair that had escaped from the topknot and resumed their lighthearted dinner conversation.

"So where did you work before coming here? You mentioned the Air Staff."

Held closely against Mac's hard body, Maggie had difficulty remembering her own name, let alone her career history. Only after she'd shifted away from the warm cradle of his thighs could she collect her thoughts.

"Mmm, yes. I worked on the Air Staff in Washington for a year or so. It was exciting, but I didn't care much for the paperwork. I decided I liked fieldwork better.

"Houston was next," she murmured into Mac's obliging shoulder. Really, it was amazing she could talk at all. She found herself reveling in the sensation of dancing with someone whose shoulder was just the right height to rest her head on. Even with her high heels, the mountain retained his majestic proportions.

"How long at Houston?" he asked, his voice low, his breath teasing the wispy curls at her ears.

"Not quite two years."

"So why did you leave there to come here? That job must have paid twice what the government could pay you."

Maggie smiled into Mac's shoulder. "I think I had this conversation once before with Ed Stockton. The same answer still holds. There's more to life than money. I wanted to get back to hands-on environmental work, and Eglin has plenty of that."

Maggie leaned back in his arms to look up at him. Mac barely managed to suppress a groan as her breasts brushed against his chest. Damn that silk! He could feel the peaks of her breasts clearly through the material, distracting him so much he almost missed her soft words.

"My needs in life are pretty simple, Mac. Some nice clothes, a good car and a challenging job, in reverse order, about sum them up."

"Isn't there something missing from that list? Like a home and a family? Someone to cook for you?" he teased.

Much as she liked him, Maggie's habit of keeping her private life private was too ingrained to give Mac anything other than the barest details.

"I've come close once or twice," she admitted lightly. "But every time I thought I'd found Mr. Right, he turned to be Mr. Wrong. Enough about me. What about you? What's on your list?"

"My priorities are pretty simple, too," Mac answered as he moved them in time to the slow dreamy tune. "The boys and the air force, not in reverse order. I'm lucky. Between those two devils and the demands of a military career, I've never been still long enough to be bored."

"And that's enough? What about someone to talk to in the night? About things besides soccer or Boy Scouts, I mean? Don't you want to marry again?"

"What makes you think husbands and wives talk in bed about anything other than Boy Scouts and grocery lists and who's going to take the kids to the dentist?"

At her mock scowl, he shrugged. "Like you, I've had a few close calls over the years. Being single and so physically big make me a real target it seems. But so far, it's just me and the boys. And Woof."

Maggie buried a small sigh of satisfaction in the fabric of Mac's shirt. She was glad Woof and the boys, and no one else, were taking up his time.

Mac led her around the dance floor a couple of more times, then leaned down to whisper in her ear, "Let's go, Maggie. I don't think I can take one more man sliding his eyes over you in that slinky getup."

Maggie gave silent thanks once more to Nieman Marcus for her outfit and smiled her readiness to leave.

She promised herself another shopping trip when Mac closed the front door of her apartment and growled, "Come here, woman. That thing you're wearing has been driving me nuts all evening."

Maggie allowed Mac's big hands to pull her close. He propped his shoulders back against the door, forcing her to put her palms on his chest and lean heavily against him. Her body was plastered against his from shoulder to knee.

"This is much better," he said, rubbing his hands up and down her back. He bent his head to taste a spot on her neck bared by the upswept curls.

Maggie kept her eyes closed. She kept her hands still where they pressed against his chest. But she couldn't keep her nipples from tightening as Mac rubbed her front against his, or a hot streak from shooting through her when his moist tongue left her neck and pushed gently into her ear.

Good grief, she thought, how did such a mountain manage to create such delicate shivers in every nook and cranny of her body? Then she forgot to think at all as his mouth took hers. He shifted her weight against his right arm. With his other hand he reached up to tug loose her curls. With a grunt of pure male satisfaction, he lifted his head to watch her hair spill down in a tumbling mass. That basic task done, he looked into her eyes.

"I want you so much it hurts, but I suspect you won't accept grits as a peace offering if I come on too strong again. So from here on out it's your call. You set the pace, Maggie. Tell me what you want."

She opened her eyes and gave him a clear direct look. "I want you, Mac. It'd be nice to get you and grits, too, but I'll settle for you."

"That's all I needed to know."

With an easy movement he bent and scooped her up in his arms, then headed down the hallway toward the bedroom.

Chapter Five

Maggie reveled in another totally new sensation as Mac carried her through the dim hall. Being carried was even more exciting than having a shoulder at just the right height to rest her head on while dancing. As best she could remember, no man had ever tried to hoist her off her feet before. *Talk* her off her feet and into bed maybe, but nothing quite this physical. She began to appreciate that there was a lot more to this seduction scene than she'd experienced before. She rather liked it, she decided, enlivening the short trip down the hall by exploring Mac's conveniently placed ear with her tongue.

Mac reacted to her explorations with satisfying directness. He dumped her on the bed with more haste than finesse and was beside her before she could catch her breath. This time his kiss was fierce and hot and demanding. Maggie kept her eyes closed once more, but now her hands roved as feverishly as his. She plucked distractedly at the buttons on his shirt, not content until she'd undone enough to slide her hands inside. Crisp hair curled over powerful chest muscles, teasing the tips of fingers. She delighted in the touch and the scent of him, strong and hard and very male.

When Mac slipped his own fingers under her satin tunic and shaped one aching breast, Maggie gasped. He slanted his mouth across hers more firmly, demanding her response. With a slow sure movement he pulled her body under his and pressed her down into the thick comforter.

"Your body fits against mine as well horizontally as it does vertically," he murmured. "I like being able to kiss most of the important spots without getting permanent spinal damage."

Maggie's breath slammed out of her as Mac suited action to words. With a quick bend of his head, he closed his mouth over a breast. She felt him hot and wet through the silk. When his teeth took the nipple and teased it into taut stiffness, a shaft of pure sensation shot through her.

He found the side button of her pants and slid them and her lace panties down to her ankles. With a muttered curse, he sat up to fumble impatiently at the tiny straps of her sandals. He finally pushed shoes, slacks and panties off in one tangled mass. Maggie reached for him and he turned back to her, but he caught both her hands loosely in one of his and stretched them over her head.

"Let me look at you, Maggie. Let me drink in the sight of those long luscious legs and gorgeous gold curls."

Maggie blushed in the half-light. She felt indescribably wanton with her lower body naked and exposed to the cool night air, not to mention his decidedly hot stare and her satin tunic sliding sensuously over highly sensitized nipples. She twisted her hands free and undid the last of his shirt buttons.

"Your turn, Mac. Let me look at you."

She pushed his shirt off shoulders so broad they blocked out all the light from the hallway when he leaned over her. Her hands fumbled at his belt buckle. With an impatient movement, he got up to rid himself of the rest of his clothes. Maggie gave in to the pleasure of watching him, then quickly pulled off her last piece of satin.

She lay back and let her eyes rove with hungry appreciation over his massive body. He fumbled in his pants pocket for a small foil package and turned away for a moment. A warm glow lodged just under her heart at his unquestioned willingness to take responsibility for her protection. When he turned back, she eyed his rampant manhood in the dim light and bit back a grin. The man certainly ran true to size!

She wondered briefly if it was possible to have too much of a good thing, then gave up all attempt at rational thought as Mac lowered himself to her side. One of his legs nudged her apart, and he slid a callused palm down her belly. His fingers tugged playfully at her nest of curls, then buried themselves in her wet heat.

Maggie arched against him. Her breathing changed to shallow panting gasps as he moved his fingers in and out, slowly, deliberately, while his thumb explored the sensitive little nub at her core. His hands tantalized and roused her to fever pitch. When he lowered his head and took an aching nipple into his mouth once more, Maggie thought she would explode.

"Not yet, Maggie my sweet," he whispered. Removing his hand, he positioned himself atop her body. "First I want to feel you all around me."

Holding her head still with both hands, watching her eyes in the dim light, Mac pushed himself into her welcoming warmth.

Long hot moments later, after his hands and his mouth and driving manhood had taken her to incredible heights of sensation, Maggie gave a hoarse cry. Waves of pleasure swamped her, and the darkness behind her closed lids shattered into splinters of bright light. Mac echoed her panting cry as her tightness gripped him in rippling waves. He muffled his shout of satisfaction against her neck and thrust deeply, following her over the edge.

Hours later, or so it seemed to Maggie, she roused herself enough to run light fingers through the dark head resting on her breast. Mashing it to a pulp, really. Even with most of his weight on his forearms, Mac crushed her into the mattress. She wiggled and tried to shift to a more comfortable position, only to have him lift his head and grin down at her.

"So soon, Maggie m'girl? Without even a nourishing snack to sustain your energy? Well, we fly-boys aim to please. If you're ready, I'll do my best."

"You big lummox, stop grinning or I might force you to make good on your boast." Maggie tried again to shift him. He let himself be moved off her body only enough to insert his hand between them and cup her breast.

"Boast? I never boast. But I need sustenance after a good workout even if you don't. I think a little midnight feeding will do it."

Before Maggie understood his meaning, he'd lowered his head and began a slow sweet suckling at her breast. His hand pushed the firm mound up so his mouth could draw at the nipple, then covered half her breast with hot wetness.

In total amazement, Maggie felt streaks of heat shoot through her again. And again, when he woke her up an hour later. Only after he'd pulled her on top of him and made her take her bedsprings to the limit of their endurance did he fall asleep himself.

She awoke again just as gray dawn was beginning to lighten the room. Without having to reach across the bed, she knew he wasn't there. She lay quietly, her eyes closed, while a series of incredibly erotic visions danced behind her eyelids. Lord, she hadn't really moaned like that, had she? Her raw throat and the tenderness between her thighs mocked her own denials.

She was about to bury her head in the covers at the thought of some of her more energetic activities when the unmistakable scent of fresh coffee reached her.

Heavens, he was domesticated, she thought. Untangling herself from the bedclothes, she slipped on the faithful short terry robe and padded down the hall to the living room. She pulled up short at the sight of Mac, slacks riding low on lean hips and shirt hanging open to display that massive chest. He was leaning casually against her desk with a steaming cup of coffee in one hand and an open folder in the other. Even from across the room, Maggie could see it was the propulsion-test folder.

The warm greeting bubbling on her lips died. Her eyes fastened on the folder in growing consternation. Was that what all this was about? Had he wined and dined and put on that admittedly spectacular bedroom performance to change her mind about that damned test? Doubts swamped her, even as Mac looked up and met her suspicious gaze.

His own slow smile of greeting died. There was no mistaking the direction of her thoughts as her eyes moved from the folder to his face. He watched her thoughtfully for a few moments, then greeted her in a neutral tone.

"Morning, Maggie."

If the woman had a problem, he wasn't going to help her with it. She could darn well spit it out.

"I see you make yourself at home, MacRae. Anything else you'd like access to? After my body and my private reports, that is?"

Whew! When she let loose, she did it with both barrels. Mac told himself to stay calm. There was nothing in this report he hadn't already seen. It was government property, for Pete's sake. Hell, he had a copy of it on his desk at work. Maggie's own people had sent it over, as she'd remember if she hadn't been so busy jumping to her angry conclusions.

Still, Mac knew he shouldn't have just picked it up and started reading while he waited for her to awake. He also knew he should apologize, but rational thought warred with stung male pride. The woman had just spent the night in his arms. How the hell could she think what she so obviously did?

Pride won. Setting his mug down with a thump that sloshed coffee over onto the damned report, he started across the room toward her. When she backed away from him nervously, he stopped short. His jaw tightened ominously.

"Dammit, Maggie, that report isn't private. I've seen it several times. It was lying open on your desk."

"The point is, it was on *my* desk, MacRae."

Even as the words tumbled from her mouth, Maggie knew she was making too much of the whole thing, but she couldn't help herself. She hadn't had that many lovers during her otherwise adventurous thirty-three years. But based on her limited experience, she thought what she and Mac had shared last night was special. It hurt to think it may not have been so special, after all, but something rather sordid. Angry and confused, she wrapped her arms around her waist.

Mac gave her a long hard look, then began buttoning his shirt.

"Fine, it's your desk. Nice to know you think I'm the kind of guy who has ulterior motives for sleeping with a woman, Maggie. You'll understand if I don't hang around for any more of your flattering comments. I have to get home before the boys wake up and put two and three together."

Miserable, Maggie stood stiff and silent as he gathered the rest of his clothes. When he let out an exasperated sigh and stopped in front of her, she set her jaw in mulish lines.

"Maggie, this is crazy. We need to talk this out."

"I don't want to talk right now," she said to the solid chest blocking her view. "Right now, all I want is for you to leave. It was fun, MacRae, but don't overstay your welcome."

Mac's breath hissed in at her flippant words. "Why the hell is it that every time we get together, it starts with magic and ends with an argument?"

When she refused to respond, he yanked the door open. "I'll talk to you later when we've both had time to cool off."

He was gone before Maggie had a chance to think of a suitably devastating response.

Chapter Six

Cool off indeed, Maggie fumed all through her quick breakfast and preparations for work. She didn't need to cool off, she needed space. Lots of it. She needed time away from a certain Colonel MacRae and his overwhelming presence. She needed...Maggie sighed and shoved the folder into her briefcase. What she needed was to put the whole incident into perspective.

It didn't help that she knew Mac was right, that she had overreacted. She felt slightly disgusted with herself as she wheeled her Jag through the crisp morning air. She knew darn well that much of her anger had stemmed from a combination of surprise and old-fashioned embarrassment. She'd never responded to any man the way she had to Mac. In the privacy of her car and her thoughts, the memory of their activities the night before still made her blush.

The early-morning drive helped her relax. It took half an hour to reach the base from her rented condo in the little resort village of Destin. The most enjoyable stretch of her drive began when she crossed the high bridge spanning the channel connecting Choctawahatchee Bay to the Gulf of Mexico. Ahead of her was Santa Rosa Island, with its rolling dunes, feathery sea oats and blinding white sand. Emerald-green gulf water sparkled on the left, while the huge bay stretched to the horizon on the right.

The sunlight dancing on the water and the smooth rush of waves washing the shore restored Maggie's usual good humor. By the time she pulled the Jag into her parking slot behind the long low World War Two-era building that held her office she had her ready smile back in place.

"Morning, team," she cheerfully greeted her small staff, who were assembled for their daily meeting. As she edged her way through the crowd in her tiny office, which had to double as a conference room, Maggie firmly suppressed a fleeting image of the spacious corner office in the Houston high-rise she'd left behind.

"Okay, we've got a lot to cover this morning. Let's start with the reds."

Within days of her arrival, Maggie and her staff had devised a color-coded system for dealing with the avalanche of issues facing them. Red signaled a potential hazard that required immediate attention to avoid danger to health or welfare; yellow, a hazard that could result in action against them by a regulatory agency but wasn't imminently threatening; blue, a task they felt needed attention but could wait; and green, a purely administrative requirement. The fact that Maggie firmly refused to waste her small overworked staff's talents on greens had won their immediate loyalty.

"We found a couple of more transformers leaking PCB last week, Maggie," said one. "I'm going out with the folks from the exterior electrical shop this morning to replace them. I'll try to get the shop to move a little faster on completing the survey."

Maggie nodded her approval. PCB, or polychlorinated biphenyl, was a highly toxic chemical compound used extensively in electrical transformers before its cancer-causing characteristics were fully understood. Eglin, like most cities across the nation, faced massive challenges in recording and replacing older transformers. The base was almost a year late in completing the survey of the hundreds of transformers used to channel power at all the test sites scattered across the half-million acres. Higher priorities had eaten away at the money and time needed for the survey, even with an extension. They only had a few more months to get it done before the extension ran out and they faced heavy fines.

"Do that, Jack. I know the shop is as strapped for manpower as we are, but we've got to get that survey done. Let me know how it goes."

An intense young woman opposite Maggie spoke up. "We found some seepage on Site 22 last week. I think it may be an abandoned underground storage area."

Maggie grimaced. Burying was the accepted method of disposing of toxic waste twenty, even ten, years ago. The nation was just beginning to understand the effects as toxic waste escaped from rusted containers and seeped into the ground. With all the tests conducted at Eglin over the years, they had dozens of known underground storage sites and probably as many that were never properly recorded.

"How bad is it?" she asked.

The woman looked at her notes. "There's a small pool of greenish liquid, with bubbling at one edge. I'm going out with the Bio-environmental folks from the hospital this morning to take samples for analysis."

Telling her she'd join them, Maggie finished her short meeting. She was on her way back from the washroom, where she'd changed her linen skirt and high heels for the jeans and rubber wading boots she kept in her office, when her intercom rang.

"Dr. Wescott, it's May in Colonel Stockton's office. The boss just got a call from the lab. They'd like you to meet with them this morning to go over the propulsion test."

"I can't do it this morning, May. See if you can set it up for this afternoon and call me back. I'll be on my beeper."

Maggie replaced the phone with a twinge of guilt. She could've rearranged her schedule. After all, the test was a top priority. But the small act of defiance somehow made her feel better about last night. With a cheerful nod to her crew, she clumped out of the office and went off to explore the green slimy gook.

When she entered the armament lab's paneled conference room later that afternoon, she was once again in her skirt. The soft cream-colored linen was paired with a gold-patterned silk blouse and high-heeled sandals. A long strand of cultured pearls gave her added dignity, she thought. She suspected she'd need all the professionalism she could muster for this meeting.

The half-dozen or so men present stood up as she entered. A couple of them, including an older distinguished-looking man who should have known better, stared outright. She wasn't quite the type of engineer they were used to dealing with, if Maggie read their assorted expressions right. Well, here we go again, she thought.

"Good afternoon, gentlemen, I'm Dr. Wescott." She moved to an empty chair on one side of the long polished table. Setting her briefcase down, she went around the room to meet each man individually. Pleasantries done, she sat down and looked inquiringly at the man who'd introduced himself as Dr. Ames, the lab's deputy director. It was their meeting, she thought. They could darn well take the lead.

The older man shook his head slightly and squared his tweed-covered shoulders. "Ah, Dr. Wescott, Colonel MacRae asked me to get the propulsion team together so we could discuss your objections to the test. I'm not sure we understand some of your concerns."

"My team's concerns were detailed in the draft report they sent over several weeks ago," Maggie responded coolly. Then, with a small sigh to herself, she relented. Ames probably hadn't even read the report. Besides, she preferred a cooperative mode of operation. "However, I appreciate the chance to discuss the project in detail with you. I understand it's an important test for Eglin, and I'm part of the team now."

"Good. We've set aside an hour for Major Hill to brief you and answer your questions."

Ames settled himself with a condescending smile into the chair at the head of the table and nodded to the young major standing by the podium. Maggie decided to ignore the pompous deputy, and turned to the man who should really know what this project was all about.

Three hours later, the once immaculate conference table was littered with coffee cups and scattered papers. Discarded suit coats lay over the backs of chairs and various charts filled a large corkboard. Major Hill had abandoned his canned briefing and was standing by a built-in blackboard, scribbling notes as the group worked their way through one particularly complex chart covered with annotations and formulas.

Mac entered the conference room through his office's connecting door. He stopped short at the sight of Maggie and his deputy bent over the table, trying to read one of the chart's more obscure formulas.

Waving the other men back into their chairs as they started to rise, he leaned against the wall and waited patiently for Maggie and Ames to finish. His eyes passed over the way the soft linen clung to her delectable tush, and he shook his head in despair. Her wardrobe was wreaking havoc with his self-control.

"Dr. Wescott."

Mac greeted her gravely when the pair finally finished examining the chart and straightened up. His firm handshake held Maggie's until she tugged it free.

"Colonel MacRae." She nodded curtly.

His small private smile gently mocked her. He held her gaze for a moment, then turned an inquiring look on his deputy.

"We're getting there, Mac," Ames responded heavily. "We've resolved most of the minor questions and are just getting into some of the major issues. Dr. Wescott has some valid concerns.''

Mac bit back a smile at his deputy's reluctant admission. Ames had been a brilliant scientist in his time, but he'd peaked a few years ago. Now that he was close to retirement, he filled his time more and more with administrative duties and less with the research that was the lab's lifeblood. Mac bet Maggie had probably given him a real run for his money.

''Good. I won't interrupt you, then. Dr. Wescott, if you would, please stop by and see me before you leave.''

Maggie tried to think of some important meeting she had pending, but Mac was gone before she could tell him he could go whistle Dixie—professionally speaking, of course.

It was several hours later when the group in the conference room finally gathered up their assorted papers. Maggie had a pounding headache and was in no mood to face Mac. She knocked irritably on his office door, then entered without waiting for an answer.

He was on the phone and waved her to one of the soft leather chairs in front of his desk. Maggie tossed her briefcase down but was too restless to sit. While Mac finished his conversation, she prowled around his roomy corner suite. It had most of the trappings of a military commander's office—the requisite set of flags, a large conference table, a computer on the credenza—but few of the plaques and memorabilia most military personnel liked to display. The only real personal touches were a small picture of Mac giving a thumbs-up in the cockpit of some sleek lethal-looking jet and a picture of him with the twins, their laughing faces surrounded by bright blue sky and a tangle of fishing tackle.

His call finished, Mac watched as she settled herself with a deliberate touch of defiance in the chair across from him. His small sigh wasn't lost on Maggie.

''I take it this isn't a good time to talk about what happened last night,'' he said.

He leaned back in his massive desk chair. It probably cost the government a fortune to build one big enough to keep from folding under his bulk, Maggie thought nastily.

"No, it's not," she snapped. "I just spent five difficult hours with the lab's best and brightest. And I'm tired."

She stopped abruptly as she remembered just why she was so tired. She hadn't gotten much sleep last night. A quick glance at Mac's glinting eyes told her he was remembering, too.

"Look, Mac. I'll do my best on this damn test. Just get off my back."

Maggie bit her lip in real chagrin. Her words conjured up another decidedly erotic memory, and hot blood crept up her cheeks. She ignored the wide grin spreading across Mac's face. She got to her feet and reached for her briefcase.

"Maggie, we need to talk."

She turned at his quiet words. "Not now, please. I'm still sorting out last night in my own mind. I know I overreacted to your reading the report this morning, and I apologize for that."

Mac felt a spear of relief in his gut. He'd worried that the damn report would stand between them like a wall. Maggie's candid apology eased his tense neck muscles, but her next words had them tightening into knots again.

"I think we've both moved too fast, Mac. We need to slow this—this relationship down a bit. Why don't you call me later in the week and we'll find a time to talk?"

Pure unaccustomed anger surged through him. He wasn't about to let her get away with this call-me-sometime crap. Not after last night. She'd given herself to him totally, and his every instinct told him she wasn't the kind of woman to do that lightly. He forgot his promise to let her set the pace. He forgot his own determination not to rush her, as he had that night in his truck. He wanted to pick her up, carry her to the couch in the corner of his office and show her just how slow she thought she could take it. Only the sight of her white face, with faint blue shadows of fatigue under her eyes, stopped him.

"All right, Dr. Wescott. You've got your reprieve. But don't kid yourself that either you or I have much control over what's happening between us. Now go home and get some sleep."

He handed her her briefcase and very nobly resisted the urge to kiss her unconscious. She left with a definite flounce of cream-colored linen.

Mac watched from his office window as she crossed the street in front of the lab and climbed into her Jag. The sleek green sports car was the number-two priority in her life, he recalled. He was thinking seriously about rearranging her priorities, not to mention her clothes and her hair and her bedcovers, when his deputy, Dr. Ames, knocked on the door.

Turning, Mac greeted the older man. "Still here, Jim? Did you get everything resolved?"

"Not quite. We're going to have to modify the test significantly. That Wescott woman is stubborn as hell."

Mac made no comment. He wasn't about to argue about Maggie with anyone.

"Ed Stockton should have known better than to let her exercise veto power over this project."

"Why?" Mac asked coolly. "I've seen her credentials. She's certainly better qualified than some of the folks we've had reviewing our proposals."

"Oh, on paper, she looks good," Ames allowed.

Mac was thinking of a few other things she looked good on, as well, such as rumpled bedclothes, when Ames's next words caught his attention.

"Don't you think it's rather coincidental that she left a plush job with a corporation that's very much against alternate energy sources to come here? And one of the first things she does is put the kibosh on our test?"

Mac regarded his deputy steadily for a long minute. "What are you implying, Jim?"

"I'm not implying anything. I just find it interesting that this particular propellant has a lot of potential for commercial use. If our test succeeds, it could cut into the oil companies' profits. Be a threat to Dr. Wescott's former employers."

"We got the draft report challenging the test over a month ago, well before Dr. Wescott's arrival. Did the final signed report differ from the draft substantially?" Mac kept his voice level, fighting his rising anger.

Ames fidgeted with his tie. "I didn't read the draft myself. Major Hill briefed me on the key points. The final report included essentially the same issues, but in much more detail. Someone put a lot more work into that final product."

"Maybe if we'd put as much effort into our initial test design, we wouldn't have the problem we have today," Mac responded. "Stay with it, Jim. Let me know how you work out the remaining issues."

When his deputy left, Mac turned back to the window. The green Jag was gone. Ames's suspicions simmered at the edges of his mind, but he refused to accept them. Instinctively he knew the laughing smiling woman that was Maggie wasn't involved in anything like what Ames hinted at. He also knew that his deputy was out of touch with current technology-sharing. Transfer of the technology developed by the air force to commercial use was a side benefit of their work. Mac knew his staff had already shared information on this particular propellant at a recent consortium of military and civilian scientists. There was enough material about it now in the public domain to preclude the big energy concerns from trying to sabotage their test.

Still, Ames had made Mac realize there was a lot he didn't know about Dr. Marguerite Wescott. Such as why she'd really left Houston. And why a woman with her credentials would be content with field-level work. They'd talked about a lot of things during dinner the previous evening, but most of it was lighthearted banter, the kind men and women engage in during the first part of any courtship dance.

After what they'd shared last night, Mac wanted to know more, a lot more. He wanted to know the woman beneath the easy smile and mop of curls. He didn't like the thought that there were still parts of Maggie he wasn't privy to. With a determined snap, Mac turned off his office lights and left.

Chapter Seven

"Hey, Maggie!"

A loud bark almost drowned the enthusiastic yell. Maggie turned to see the twins waving energetically from the other side of the small cove. She waved back, then waited while Woof bounded toward her along the narrow strip of beach, with Davey—or was it Danny?—dragging behind on his leash. The other twin and a short stout woman followed in their sandy wake.

"Ugh, hello, Woof." Maggie tried to keep the massive paws off her chest and the wet slurping tongue off her face. She held him at arm's length while Davey/Danny struggled to reduce the dog's ecstatic greeting to a wagging tail, though even that furious action threatened to knock them both over.

"Whatcha doin' here? This is our favorite spot. Woof loves the water, but Dad says we can't let him loose where people go, so we always come here."

"I can understand why." Maggie smiled down at the boys while she held her shirtfront out with both hands to shake off the wet sand. Splotchy paw prints decorated the once pristine white cotton.

"I'm here checking some erosion along the shore, and no, I didn't know it was your favorite spot."

"Mrs. Harris, this is Maggie Westlake. Remember, we told you? She likes grits." The boys knew their manners, even if they couldn't remember names.

"Maggie Wescott." She smiled at the older woman and held out her hand. As her fingers were encased in a hard grip, Maggie suddenly remembered Mac's saying his housekeeper was a former prison warden. Clearly this was she.

"Hello, Dr. Wescott. Colonel Mac mentioned he had dinner with you last week."

If the older woman knew that the dinner date had lasted until morning, her bland expression gave no sign. Nevertheless, Maggie felt a surge of self-consciousness as the woman's bright eyes assessed her from head to toe.

Luckily she was spared the necessity of answering when one of the twins tugged on her sleeve.

"You wanna come with us, Maggie? We've got a special place down the beach and nobody knows about it 'cept us and Mrs. Harris. We'll show you some real neat stuff."

Maggie glanced at her watch. After a long morning in her deserted office catching up on paperwork, she'd intended to spend a few hours checking for herself the erosion along Eglin's north shoreline. She'd become so absorbed in taking notes and clambering over uprooted tree stumps that she'd forgotten the time. It was too late now for the errands she'd planned to run this beautiful Saturday afternoon. Tossing aside her plans, she gave herself up to the boys' bubbly companionship.

"Sure, I'd love to see something special. If you guys and Mrs. Harris don't mind sharing it."

"Nah, she doesn't mind, do ya?"

The older woman's plump face lost its blandness when she smiled down with genuine affection at the twins. "No, I don't mind at all. Why don't you two and Woof lead the way?"

Maggie admired the woman's strategy as the boys and Woof charged down the beach, wildly splashing through the shallows. She fell in beside Mrs. Harris, and they followed at a more leisurely pace.

"We walk along this beach almost every afternoon," the older woman said. "I thought it would take some of the edge off their collective energy, but the air and the water only seem to revive them after a tough day at school. They especially love coming here on weekends when they don't have homework hanging over their heads. My name's Kate, by the way."

"Please, call me Maggie. The boys do."

"Yes, I noticed. They talked a lot about you after the soccer game last weekend." Kate cast her a shrewd look. "They like you. So does Colonel Mac, unless I miss my guess."

Maggie blinked at the woman's bluntness. She bit back the quick retort that evidently the colonel didn't like her all that much. He hadn't called in five and a half days—not that she was counting.

"I like the boys, too. They're lively and bright."

The woman beside her snorted. "Too lively on occasion. It's a good thing I've still got my nightstick. It's the one souvenir I took with me into retirement. I keep it hanging on a very prominent peg in the kitchen. So far, just the threat of it has worked."

Maggie chuckled, then asked, "How long have you been with them?"

"Well, I came down here a couple of years ago. I'd just retired from the Federal Bureau of Prisons and thought I'd just laze the rest of my days away in the sun. That lasted about a week. Luckily, Colonel Mac advertised for a housekeeper about the time I started counting damp spots on the walls for entertainment."

By the time they caught up with the twins, Kate had Maggie laughing delightedly with stories of her days "in the pen," as she termed it.

"C'mon, Maggie, look here!"

Two pairs of excited blue eyes and two very wide grins told her this was the special place. Maggie looked around the small cove with interest. A fallen tree edged the bank and scrub littered the narrow beach, but try as she might, Maggie couldn't see what held their interest.

"Here, right here."

Danny, yes, she was sure it was Danny, pointed. He was the one with the single dimple in one freckled cheek. He grabbed hold of her hand and together they waded toward the north end of the cove, where the water of the bay lapped right up against the rugged shore. It wasn't until they were almost upon it that Maggie noticed the indentation halfway down the bank.

"It's a cave. Dad says Indians used to camp here in the old days. This was one of their hiding places. See, it goes way back behind the bushes and has all kinds of neat stuff in it."

Danny pulled her closer to the hole and bent his body half into the shadowed darkness. Maggie resisted the urge to pull him out. So far she hadn't seen any snakes or wild creatures in the area, but she didn't much care for dark holes, inhabited or otherwise.

"There're bunches of arrowheads in there and some old pot bits," Davey explained while his brother continued to root around in the cave. Danny emerged, grimy but triumphant, gripping some small stones. He took Maggie's hand and poured them into her palm. Sure enough, they were arrowheads.

Maggie didn't know much about archaeology, but she did know that northwest Florida has been home to several prehistoric tribes. They'd hunted the vast forests and fished the rich waters of Choctawahatchee Bay. In fact, the bay was named for one of the early tribes. There were several major historical sites and hundreds of minor finds scattered across the Eglin complex.

Her staff had briefed her about the consultant from Florida State University who was on call for archaeological matters. He was supposed to help catalog finds and do the necessary paperwork whenever there was any test activity that might affect a historical site.

"Dad says we can't take them 'cause they have to be registered or something. But we can play with them if we're careful."

Maggie knew there was a whole storeroom of as yet uncataloged artifacts somewhere on base. But archaeological-consultant fees ranked low on the list of the base's priorities.

"Go ahead, look inside and see how many there are."

"Ah, no, thanks, Davey. I'll take your word for it." No way was she going to stick her head or any other part of her anatomy into that hole.

"Chicken!" Dave taunted over Maggie's laughing protests. His twin took up the refrain, with enthusiastic accompaniment from Woof. Mrs. Harris added her voice to the general cacophony, telling the boys to lay off. Then a deep voice interrupted them all.

"You have to learn to take a lady at her word when she says no, boys."

"Dad! You're home."

The boys scooted up the bank, Woof at their heels, and threw themselves at their father. Mac wrapped a big arm around each of them, only to let go to ward off Woof's happy greeting. The boys shouted with laughter when Woof managed to sneak in a wet swipe at their father's face on one of his bouncing tries.

Maggie watched the four of them. Whatever else the exasperating man might be, he was a good parent. Their unabashed joy in each other shone through like a beacon.

She and Mrs. Harris climbed the slight bank as Mac finally calmed dog and boys.

"Hello, Kate. I expected to find you and the boys here, but I didn't expect to find you had company."

Maggie sucked in her breath as the corners of Mac's mouth pulled up in a slow easy smile. Damn, one smile and he could make her forget five and a half days without a call—almost.

She started to return his greeting, only to lose his attention to a demanding nine-year-old.

"Did you fly the F-15 back, Dad? Did you? How'd it handle?"

"Yes, Dave, I flew it back. And it was worth waiting a week for. It cuts through the air like the Eagle it's named for. Come on back to the house and I'll tell you all about it." He ruffled the boy's hair, then turned to Maggie.

"Why don't you come back with us? I smelled something delicious when I passed through the kitchen on my way out here." His twinkling eyes told her he knew very well she could resist *him,* but probably not the offer of food.

"Yeah, please come, Maggie," said Davey. "Mrs. Harris made lasagna. You'll like it better'n grits, even."

"How can I pass up an offer like that? But I left my car parked back up the beach. I better go get it."

"We'll go with you, so we can show you the way."

The boys slithered eagerly back down the bank. Mac managed to grab Woof's collar just in time to keep him from joining them. He could just see Maggie driving down the road with a big hairy hound sticking out of the sunroof of her Jag.

"See you at the house." He smiled and turned to join a very interested Mrs. Harris.

By the time Maggie made it back to her car, answered the boy's excited questions about just how fast the Jag could go and followed their somewhat disjointed directions to their bay-front home, she'd managed to get a few questions of her own answered. So Mac had left unexpectedly for California to participate in some special test at Edwards Air Force Base. So he just got back this afternoon. So maybe that was why he hadn't called....

Chapter Eight

Three hours, two helpings of lasagna and a long laugh-filled game of Monopoly later, Mrs. Harris sent the protesting twins to bed. She went upstairs herself soon after, with only one or two significant glances and a slightly smug grin.

Mac poured brandy into large snifters and led Maggie out of the cluttered den to the deck that ran the entire length of the back of the big house. The last rays of the sun streaked through dark clouds drifting above the bay. With a contented sigh, Maggie slouched down in a redwood lounge piled with weather-beaten cushions and stretched her long jean-covered legs out to rest on the deck rail. Woof immediately plunked his massive head down on her knees. Two soulful eyes gazed up at her in the dim light until she got the message and began to scratch behind his ears.

"I'm sorry I didn't get a chance to call before I left for California. I didn't like leaving things unsettled between us. I thought the conference would never end."

Maggie turned her head to study the man next to her. He was as relaxed as she in a huge battered chair. His face was hard to see in the fading light, but she could feel his eyes watching her.

"It was a long week for me, too, Mac." Her admission surprised her. "I half expected you to call to make sure Ames and I hadn't killed each other trying to resolve the rest of the test questions.'' She could see his white teeth as he smiled in the gathering darkness.

''Well, *you're* still alive. Is he?''

''Barely. The man is more stubborn than I am. We still haven't closed on one or two issues,'' Maggie warned softly. ''If we don't resolve them this week, you may have to scrub the test.''

''To tell you the truth, I'm sick and tired of that damn test,'' Mac grumbled. ''I'm still carrying the scars from your raking me over when you found me reading your report. I was hurt by your thinking I'd had an ulterior motive for sleeping with you.''

''I'm sorry, Mac,'' Maggie murmured as she swirled the brandy around in the heavy crystal goblet and scratched Woof's shaggy head absently. ''I knew there wasn't a thing in that folder you hadn't already seen, but I was too upset to admit it. I'm not normally a suspicious person. I don't know what it is about you, about us, that makes me overreact so.''

Mac grinned at her. ''I've noticed that your emotions do run a bit high. Seems like every time we've been together, I've had to beat a hasty retreat. That's not a very satisfactory state of affairs for a military man.''

''Well, why don't we declare a truce?'' she asked lightly.

''Nope. No truce. A truce implies both parties shake hands, retire from the field of honor and go their separate ways.''

''A cease-fire, then? An end to hostilities.''

''Not good enough. Nothing so imprecise for us.''

''Well, for heaven's sake, what *do* you want?'' Maggie asked, exasperated.

''I won't settle for anything less than unconditional surrender.''

Maggie bristled. She'd been her own woman too long and was too comfortable in her independence to accept his casual ultimatum.

"Whose surrender? Yours or mine?"

"What difference does it make?" Mac asked with a low chuckle. "If it matters, I give!"

He rose, then reached down to pull Maggie to her feet. Taking the glass from her suddenly nerveless fingers, he sat back on the rail and pulled her between his legs. Maggie gave a devout prayer that the railing was up to holding his weight before he tugged her head down to meet his.

A loud slurping sound brought them both back to consciousness long moments later.

"Woof, for Pete's sake, get away from that brandy!"

Mac eased her out of his arms to move toward the dog. Pulling a crystal goblet off the end of a long hairy nose, he shooed the grinning hound into the house.

Maggie waited silently in the dark while he tended to the dog, using the brief respite to try to settle her spinning senses.

"Come on, I'll take you home." His shape materialized beside her in the dark.

"You don't need to. My car's here."

Mac took her chin in his fingers and turned her face up to his. "We'll come back for it in the morning."

If there was a question in his words, Maggie didn't hear it. She heard only quiet conviction.

"You've filled my mind all week, Maggie. When I saw you with the boys this afternoon there on the beach, I felt like I'd truly come home. I've been aching to hold you in my arms all evening. Let me take you home."

With a sense that she was committing herself to something she wasn't quite ready for, something deeper and stronger than she'd ever felt before, Maggie nodded slowly.

With that nod, she knew she'd crossed a line, one she'd had in front of her throughout her varied personal and professional life. She'd always kept things light and kept herself on the move. Even the upwardly mobile and short-lived fiancé hadn't drawn the unspoken commitment from her Mac had. In fact, one of the main reasons she'd left Houston was to distance herself from the man who'd started pressuring her to put down roots, to take her position in the corporate world more seriously. Yet here she was, less than two weeks after meeting Mac, driving through the dark to a night of loving in his arms. Throughout the long trip back to her condo, she wondered just who had surrendered to whom back there on the deck.

As they rolled silently through the glowing Florida moonlight, Mac, too, examined his feelings, trying to understand the fierce satisfaction he felt to have this tousled, exasperating, wholly fascinating creature beside him. When he'd seen her there on the beach, laughing with the boys, a sense of absolute certainty had jolted through him. He wanted this woman—in his bed and in his life. Tonight he'd try to make her want him, too.

He smiled when he closed her condo door behind them. She stood uncertainly in the middle of her living room, looking at him with a slight frown.

"Don't worry so, Maggie. I won't ask anything of you you're not prepared to give."

"Damn that smile," Maggie said with a resigned sigh as she walked into his open arms. "It constitutes a lethal weapon."

Mac let her set the pace as she explored his lips. He contented himself with running his hands over the rear so obligingly at arm's reach and available to him in the tight jeans.

His smug confidence that he could control the pace shattered when she ran her hands down his chest, then lower still. When they moved slowly, deliberately, over his manhood, Mac sucked in a quick breath and pulled her hands away. Maggie tugged them free and went back to her erotic massage. The bulge in his jeans turned rock hard under her hands. Mac stood it as long as he dared, then groaned and pulled her hands away once more, this time twisting her arms behind her back and holding them there with a gentle grip.

"Maggie," he said on a shuddering breath.

"Don't worry, Mac," she looked up at him with a teasing glint in her green eyes. "I won't ask for anything you're not prepared to give."

That did it. With a low growl, Mac had her flat on her back on the soft carpet. Her arms were still twisted behind her back, causing her breasts to arch up invitingly toward him. Mac gave her a mocking smile that promised retribution, then bent his head and took one nipple into his mouth, his teeth worrying it until it grew hard. Maggie gasped as he continued to nip and suck at her aching breast through the soft cotton shirt. She tried to free her hands.

"Oh, no, Maggie m'girl. Not yet. I owe you for that little bit of teasing."

Mac pushed one heavy leg between hers and used it to pry her thighs apart. His free hand roamed down her front, to the deep jean-covered V between her legs. Maggie held her breath as he cupped her mound and ran his fingers along the seam of her jeans. She felt the heat of his hand even through the thick material. And it felt wonderful.

Mac, too, could feel her heat. For a few moments more he struggled to hold on to his own control as his hand shaped and stroked her femininity. He bent down to still her thrashing head and capture her soft moans in his mouth. All vestiges of playfulness disappeared. He gave in to the deep primal need of the male to cover his mate.

Maggie lay helpless as he released her arms and methodically removed both her clothes and his own. He made undressing a new erotic experience as his mouth touched everywhere his hands uncovered. By the time he had taken the few seconds to protect her and had repositioned himself at the juncture of her thighs, she barely had the strength to lift her legs around his waist as he directed. Mac tried to cushion her on his arms as he moved into her in long sure thrusts. Her back was spared, but her hips ground against the carpet with every move.

Mac took a handful of soft curly hair in both fists and held her head steady so he could look down into her face. He could tell by her soft moans and the gathering spasms of her satiny sheath that she was near her peak. For some reason, it was vitally important to see her face when he brought her to pleasure. Only after she'd arched under him and he'd seen, as well as felt, her shattering climax, did he allow himself to close his eyes and follow her over the edge.

Chapter Nine

"Well, I see the mountain has come to Muhammad," Ed Stockton tossed at her with a grin several weeks later. They'd just finished a meeting on a new education center to be built on base. Unfortunately the chosen site was right in the middle of a nesting area for red-cockaded woodpeckers, one of Eglin's endangered species. The meeting had been lively, to say the least, and Ed was glad it was over so he could turn to more interesting matters.

Maggie didn't pretend to misunderstand his sly comment. She stopped gathering up her papers to grin back at him. "Let's just say we met on the road to Mecca."

Ed had teased her once or twice about her pet name for Mac—the mountain—since the rumors began that she was seeing the lab commander on other than business. This was the first time she'd acknowledged their relationship publicly.

"The word is you and MacRae are making all the local hot spots together, kiddo."

"What there are of them," Maggie laughed back. In addition to the various official functions on base Mac had taken her to, they had explored the rich fare in their corner of northwest Florida. Under the twins' enthusiastic tutelage, Maggie had been given a crash course in the local haute cuisine.

Quick visions of restaurants with paper place mats and plastic baskets piled high with shrimp and mouth-watering fried amberjack filled Maggie's mind. Mac had taken them all out to various local eateries, seeming to derive as much enjoyment from watching Maggie and the boys together as from the food itself. Mrs. Harris enjoyed the treats, too. She ate the local fare heartily, but insisted they all go "home" for dessert. Somewhere in her long career she had picked up a fatal weakness for gooey, saccharine-sweet confections, and always had something freshly baked in the pantry. Maggie and Mac discreetly scraped off layers of frothy icing and passed the goo to an appreciative Woof rather than dampen Kate's pride in her culinary achievements.

But the desserts were nothing compared to the sweetness that followed when Mac drove Maggie home. When it wasn't too late, when one or the other of them didn't have an early conference or a flight, or the boys weren't expecting him back, Mac would stay the night and they would make long lingering love. Other times, when he couldn't stay, they shared more kisses and heavy breathing than anything else.

"Jim Ames was over here yesterday. He mentioned that their big test is set for next week." Ed Stockton's voice interrupted Maggie's private thoughts. She frowned.

"Yes, I know. It was a struggle getting them to agree to all our conditions. The last issue was the height of the dike around the ignition site. Mac approved the change—and the associated costs—over Ames's objections."

"Ames was also asking a lot of rather strange questions," Ed continued after a pause. "Like why you left a big oil conglomerate to come to this little corner of God's country. Particularly when we're about to test a new energy source that might make your former employers very, uh, nervous."

Maggie stiffened and turned slowly to face her boss. She let the implications of what he was saying sink in fully before she answered.

"And what did you tell him."

Ed blinked at the ice in her voice. "Hey, hold on there. Don't shoot the messenger. I told Ames he was nothing but a fussy old woman— Oops, sorry!"

Ed had a tendency to forget that some of the old euphemisms were taboo in the current more sensitive work environment. Maggie usually didn't hesitate to correct any of her crusty old boss's lapses, but this one she let slide.

"I just thought you'd want to know what you're dealing with."

Maggie gave him a hard clear look, then nodded. She walked back through the bustling yard to her office, for once not noticing the activity teeming around her.

Industrial espionage—that's what the old fart was implying. She thought indignantly of all the hours she'd humored the man, maintaining a polite respectful demeanor even when he asked the same question for the third or fourth time. Despite herself, she couldn't help wondering whether Mac knew of Ames's suspicions. Surely, he himself didn't think that about her, not after all they'd shared.

Mac came by early that evening to pick her up for a formal function at the base. He could tell something was wrong as soon as she opened the door. She'd caught her hair up with glittering rhinestone combs, and was wearing a long slinky red thing that almost covered her tall frame, except for the slit up one side that appeared to go all the way to her armpit. It was an outfit only someone with Maggie's long lithe beauty could carry off, and one that made Mac's mouth go dry. The look that should have gone with that getup was sultry and smiling. Instead, there was a slight furrow on Maggie's brow, quickly erased as she took in his full glory.

"Lord, Mac. I didn't think they made uniforms with padded shoulders like that," she teased.

"It's the shoulder boards. And this damn cummerbund. They make a man look like he's all trussed up."

Not hardly, Maggie thought, as she feasted on the sight of Mac in his dress uniform. The short tailored jacket of midnight blue sported a glittering array of medals, topped by shiny wings. It fastened with a single button at his trim waist, showing a deeper blue cummerbund, pleated white dress shirt and a jaunty satin bow tie.

"Is this the same man whose standard dress is worn jeans and old sweatshirts?" she asked with an awe that was only half-pretended.

"One and the same, Maggie m'girl. I'll prove it."

And he did, with a kiss that left them both breathless. Maggie was still trying to steady her racing pulses when he put a finger under her chin and tilted up her head.

"Your dress is spectacular—what there is of it—and I love your hair up. The only thing missing is the smile in your eyes. What's the matter?"

Maggie wasn't ready to talk to him about Ed Stockton's disclosures, nor the doubts they raised in her. Not now, with a big function ahead of them. Later, she thought. Later they'd talk.

"Nothing, Mac. I'm a little nervous about tonight's do, I guess. I haven't been to one of these before."

The Maggie he knew wasn't nervous about anything. Mac decided not to press the issue until they had time to thrash out whatever was bothering her. Later, he thought.

"Don't get your hopes up, honey," he warned as he escorted her outside. In honor of the occasion he'd brought his little sports car instead of the Jeep. "The Air Force isn't very old. We're the baby military service, don't forget. We're still feeling our way between ironclad British-mess traditions and fighter-pilot free-for-alls. What you'll see tonight will probably be a mixture of the best and the worst of both."

His words proved prophetic. Maggie couldn't remember ever attending any function where dignitaries were marched to a noxious-looking grog bowl for real or imagined slights. Everyone forgot the rules of the mess in the general hilarity and camaraderie that filled the ballroom. She laughed at the silly rituals and was moved to tears by the guest speaker. The former POW spoke quietly about his experiences in Vietnam. Looking around the room during his stark moving speech, Maggie noted fierce feelings of pride on the faces of the men and women in uniform as they listened to their comrade-in-arms. With a rush of indefinable emotion, she took in Mac's clenched jaw and intense eyes. The speaker finished with a simple prayer for the warriors left behind.

Mac held her close against him as they danced after the official part of the evening ended. Even when the music sped up and the younger couples around them gyrated across the floor, he held her close and moved to his own beat. They were among the last to leave.

If Maggie thought the long dinner, the numerous toasts and the intimate dancing had made Mac forget her earlier pensiveness, she soon learned her mistake. When the door of her condo closed behind them, he led her over to an armchair and sat down, pulling her onto his lap.

She was going to have to invest in some sturdier furniture, Maggie thought as the chair creaked ominously under them.

"Okay, now tell me why your eyes have had a shadow in them all night."

She looked up at him, surprised. She hadn't even thought of Ames's ugly insinuations for whole hours at a stretch tonight. How in the world had Mac seen through her laughter and tears to the worry beneath? She took a deep breath. Better to get it out than let it fester. Besides, it wasn't her nature to dissemble or hide her feelings for long.

"Ed Stockton told me Dr. Ames seems to think I have some ulterior motive in my objections to the propulsion test. Something to do with loyalty to my former employer."

Mac cursed his bumbling deputy roundly. "Ames is a fool, Maggie. You probably talked circles around him, and he reached for something to justify his own inadequacies. The test is a go for next week, isn't it?"

She nodded, a troubled frown creasing her brow.

"My people resolved every one of your objections, didn't they?"

She nodded again. "I had my deputy review the proposed changes, as well—he's the one who wrote the original draft report. He's satisfied with the new parameters."

"So that proves you're not trying to sabotage the effort." Mac ran his thumb lightly along her furrowed brow. "Don't let Ames's dithering bother you."

Maggie let her breath out on a ragged sigh. "I'll be glad when the darn thing's done. It seems as if this test has been hanging over us forever." Swallowing, she looked up at him. "It's still awfully dangerous, Mac."

"That's the nature of the test business," he reminded her quietly. "You know that as well as I do. We're pushing the edge of the envelope, stretching into the unknown with every new plane we take up, every new chemical or explosive we test. All we can do is ensure all possible safety factors are considered."

Maggie huddled against Mac's solid chest. She wanted desperately to believe his steady measured words. Normally she wouldn't have let a man like Ames bother her in the least. She had supreme confidence in herself and her professionalism. But she felt vulnerable lately, as if by giving in to Mac, she was laying open a part of herself that had been hers alone up till now. Her confidence had developed a soft spot where he or anything to do with him was concerned.

"Look at me, Maggie," Mac's quiet voice commanded. "I refuse to let you be bothered by Ames. Forget it. Forget him!"

Maggie couldn't hold back a smile at his crisp order. "Yes, sir!" She tried to sit at attention in his lap and give him a smart salute.

Mac groaned as her fanny wiggled against him and held her still. They both forgot Ames and the lab and the test and their own names for a good long time.

In fact, Maggie managed to push the propulsion test to the back of her mind. She'd done everything required by law or common sense to protect the environment and the people involved, and had other equally demanding projects to occupy her energies. Added to her pressure at work, Mac had given her some more things to fill her mind, not to mention her body and her heart. He'd begun to get downright grumpy about the evenings he couldn't stay with her and had to leave for his own home. And in a man as big and normally even-tempered as Mac, grumpy was definitely a state to be reckoned with.

"Something's got to give, woman. I don't like crawling out of your bed and sneaking back into my home like an adolescent."

Mac nudged Maggie out of her sleepy lethargy and settled her boneless body in the crook of his arm. She snuggled into his warmth contentedly, wishing he'd let her just drift off to sleep. They'd had this discussion several times already.

"I love you, Maggie."

That got her attention. Her heavy lashes fluttered open to find him staring down at her, a determined expression in his eyes.

"I hate leaving you at night. I want us together, in our own bed, every night. I think we should get married."

As proposals go, Maggie had had better, but none that tempted her as much. None that called out to her heart to grab hold of something permanent, something wonderful. She wanted desperately to say yes.

"I... I think we should think about it." She forced herself to meet Mac's eyes. "I think I love you, too, Mac. But I've thought I was in love before, and it didn't work out. We owe it to the boys to take this slowly."

Mac's eyes narrowed. "Don't use the boys as an excuse. This is between us. And what's between us deserves better than this sneaking around. I want to marry you."

Some of Maggie's independence reasserted herself. After all, it was her bed and her bedroom and her life.

"You need to work on your technique, Colonel. Men usually ask women to marry them, not order them." She tried to slip out of bed to put some distance between them.

"Oh, no, you don't." Mac pulled her back easily. "I want an answer, however the question was or wasn't phrased."

"I told you, I need to think about it!" she snapped. At his hurt look, Maggie relented. "Mac, you don't understand. I... I'm nervous about marriage. I came really close once, and when I did, a trapped feeling overwhelmed me and I bolted at the last minute. I left a good job in Houston because I just wasn't ready and my fiancé was."

Well, at least now he knew why she'd come to Eglin, Mac thought. For a long moment, he studied her. He knew her too well to think she was being coy. It hurt him more than he was prepared to admit that she had doubts when he had none at all. He'd known she was the one he wanted in his home and his heart from the moment he'd seen her up to her knees in water, poking in that dark hole with the boys.

"Okay," he said finally, levering himself off the rumpled bed. "Think about it. But think hard, Maggie m'girl. I may be big, but I'm not particularly slow or patient."

He reached down, took a handful of her hair in one fist and held her steady for his kiss. When he left, closing the door carefully behind him, he was breathing as fast and as painfully as she was.

Chapter Ten

Maggie was learning. She followed Mac's orders and thought hard over the next few days. She remembered her feelings of panic when her former fiancé had pressured her, although not quite as forcefully as the mountain had. She remembered how she'd run from him and her Houston job to escape her feelings of being trapped. And she compared those feelings to the intense urge she felt to accept Mac's hand and heart.

She didn't feel trapped with Mac, she felt…confused. Ten years or more of lighthearted wandering wherever her will and her talents took her were at stake. Suddenly they seemed trivial compared to what she suspected she might find with Mac and his two, correction, three, holy terrors.

Maggie had just tossed another page of doodles into her overflowing wastebasket when the crash phone rang. With Eglin's active flying mission, there were usually one or two in-flight emergencies a day, most of which ended routinely. Maggie or one of her staff monitored every call on the crash line. If the incident being reported turned out to be serious, they needed to respond. She picked up the receiver quickly.

"This is the Eglin command post. We have a report of an explosion on the range. The base commander has directed the disaster-response team to assemble immediately at Base Operations. Acknowledge."

Maggie's heart turned over in her chest. Telling herself not to panic, she waited until the command post rapped out her office code, then responded with the approved call sign.

Don't let it be the propulsion test! Dear Lord, please don't let it be the test! Her mind screamed the silent prayer as she grabbed her boots and jeans, slammed her office door shut and tore off her skirt and slip. Her fingers trembled, fumbling on the snaps. She grabbed her hard hat and was just pulling the thick disaster-response team checklist out of the bookcase when her intercom rang. She started to ignore it, but a quick glance told her it was Ed Stockton's direct line.

"Maggie, we just got a call. There's been an explosion."

She sucked in her breath. "Yes, I know. I just took the notification from the command post. I'm on my way out the door."

"Did they tell you the location or nature of the accident?"

"No." Maggie's last hope died at Ed's flat hard tone.

"It was Site 32. The propulsion test. Something went wrong."

"I was afraid it was," she rasped out. "Ed, Mac's out there!"

And Jack, her deputy, along with a lot of other people, she thought. She swallowed her gut-wrenching fear. Gripping the phone so hard her hand hurt, she forced herself to ask. "Any report of casualties?"

"Not yet. The fire department's on the scene right now. The chief himself went out for this one. He'll do whatever's necessary until the disaster-response team gets there."

Ed's words recalled Maggie with a jerk. "I've got to go. The team's assembling at Base Ops now. I've got our van with the radio in it. Please, please, let me know if you hear anything."

She knew the fire chief would be in direct contact with Ed, probably before he even called the command post to update them.

"Will do, Maggie. Be careful, okay? You know better than anyone how dangerous this may be."

She didn't need that reminder, Maggie thought as she forced herself to drive the speed limit the short distance to Base Ops. She knew it would take longer for the rest of the team to arrive, some coming from the hospital all the way on the west side of the base.

Please let Mac be okay, she prayed over and over in an unconscious litany. *Let me see him again.* They hadn't been together since Mac had delivered his marriage proposition three nights ago. Maggie refused to call it a proposal—it had really been more of a command—but it had filled her mind almost to the exclusion of everything else. She rubbed her eyes with a fist to hold back the threat of tears.

Forcing her personal fears from her mind, she made herself focus on her professional responsibilities. Mentally she reviewed everything she knew about the test. She'd gone over it with Jack again just this morning. Since he'd done the original analysis and wanted to cover the actual test, she'd agreed. Maggie refused to give in to the sick guilt that threatened to swamp her. She should have gone out to the test site, instead of Jack. He knew the test, knew all the properties of the chemicals they were using, knew the dangers. But it was her responsibility. And Mac may be hurt.

By the time she reached Base Ops and unloaded her gear, she had forced herself to an icy calm. She'd practiced with the disaster-response team a couple of times since coming to Eglin. The team took their responsibilities with deadly seriousness. Their practices were frighteningly realistic. They had to be. Eglin had an active flying mission and the population of a medium-sized city. Any type of accident could happen, from gas-main explosions to fires to airplane crashes. The exercise-team chief enlisted schoolchildren, wives and on-base civilians as participants in simulated bus crashes, hostage situations and major explosions of all types. Hospital personnel painted gory injuries on the players. The more realistic the better.

Their practice stood them in good stead now. As the various team members assembled, they ran through their checklists with brisk efficiency. The on-scene commander briefed them on what he knew, which wasn't much more than what had been relayed by the command post. Each team member then described what he or she knew of the test and the site. Maggie forced herself to detail calmly the environmental hazards to the other team members. Everything inside her wanted to scream at them to get on with it, to move faster. Her rational mind knew the danger of plunging blindly into an accident site. But emotionally, she wished she could jump in her van and take off without waiting.

After what seemed like hours, but was only minutes, the on-scene commander directed the team to an entry control/safe point coordinated by radio with the fire chief. Maggie ran to her van, accompanied by the chaplain and two bioenvironmental techs. Her four-wheeler could handle the rough range roads easily. She wheeled the van into the convoy of vehicles that drove off the main base, led by a police car with its siren screaming.

She kept the radio tuned to the fire-station crash line all during the long ride to the site. The firefighters were real pros, and the chief especially so. He kept chatter over the open radio to a minimum. Their lines were unscrambled and often monitored by civilians off base. There was no need to panic the general populace until they knew the scope of the disaster.

"It's Jack. Thank God!"

Maggie all but shouted as her van pulled up to the circle of police cars and fire trucks gathered at the entry-control point. Even from a distance she recognized her tall bearded deputy. Before the van had completely stopped rolling, Maggie slammed it into park and leapt out. As she ran toward Jack, she could hear the roar of flames and smell the sharp acrid scent of smoke in the air. Tall pines blocked the accident scene from sight.

"Jack, are you okay?" She grabbed his arm.

"I'm fine, boss. I wasn't on-site when it happened. I'd just come back to my car for some notes I needed."

"What happened? How bad is it?"

"It wasn't the propellant, Maggie. The stuff hadn't even been unloaded from the containers."

Maggie clutched his arm hard in relief. All during the long drive to the site, she'd dreaded hearing reports of toxic clouds spreading over the area.

"It was some kind of a freak accident. The crane lifting the firing tube into place snapped a cable, which in turn whipped into the mechanized loading vehicle. From what I can gather, sparks ignited the vehicle's fuel and caused the explosion. I wasn't there, though. The fire chief has the real poop."

Maggie glanced over to where the chief was briefing the on-scene commander. She turned back and asked the question eating at her soul.

"Jack, did you see Colonel MacRae before or after the accident?"

Jack shook his head slowly. He, like most of the engineering squadron, knew Maggie was dating the lab commander. Maggie caught back a ragged sob, then made herself take several deep breaths.

"The chief might know something," Jack volunteered. "He just came out of the accident area a few minutes ago."

Maggie knew she couldn't interrupt the fire chief as he huddled with the on-scene commander, but she watched them closely. When the commander turned away to take a radio call, she approached the sweating helmeted fireman.

"Chief, Colonel MacRae was supposed to be on-site for the test. Have you had contact with him?"

The stocky grizzled man turned to face Maggie. He admired and respected this vibrant young woman. She'd ridden with his fire crews during a couple of exercises and had spent a full day with his hazardous-materials team. If Maggie's own credentials hadn't already won his professional respect, her willingness to listen and learn from his people would have done it.

"Sorry, Dr. Wescott. I haven't seen him. There's still a lot of confusion in there." He nodded toward the flames they could see leaping above the treeline. "We should hear something soon."

He turned away to answer a call from the on-scene commander. They talked for a moment, then the commander called his team together. Maggie knew the man in charge both personally and professionally. She and Mac had been seated beside him and his wife at more than one social function. Maggie gave grateful thanks that he'd been in the job for more than two years and knew his stuff.

"Okay, this is what we have so far," the commander said. "A vehicle fire and explosion occurred just north of the control center at Site 32. Burning fuel sprayed several workers in the area. The fire crews have stabilized at least two people with severe burns, but there may be more."

He nodded to the senior medical rep. "Doc, make sure your folks call back for more burn-trauma kits, just in case. Additionally, the fuel ignited both structural and brush-fires that are still burning. The lab folks moved the propellant and main rocket fixtures off-site immediately and they're out of range. Thank God we don't have that to worry about. But there may be other chemicals stored or brought out for the test. Fire crews are surveying the area now."

He took a deep breath, then finished with, "There were several lab and range control crews on-site. We're trying to get a firm head count. I'm going in with the chief now. Doc, you better come with me. The rest of you wait until I call you in."

Maggie bit her lip in an agony of frustration. Now that her worst fears of a major chemical disaster were allayed, every nerve and fiber in her body screamed for word of Mac. She forced herself to review again her disaster-response checklist, going over the sections on chemical and natural fires. Together, she and Jack added to the grease-pencil annotations on the checklist. She'd have to either call or fax a detailed report to both state and federal environmental agencies as soon as the imminent danger passed.

"Dr. Wescott, over here, please. Major, you, too."

Maggie looked up to see the on-scene commander returning. She and the senior bio-environmental medical engineer hurried over.

"Look, there are some barrels burning close to the control center. We couldn't find any lab folks who knew what they contained. The senior test engineer is one of those seriously injured. The chief has what markings his people could get off the barrels. I need you to get with him immediately and see if you can figure out if we have a danger of a secondary explosion on our hands."

Maggie and the young major hurried over to the worried fire chief. "What do we have?"

"I think they're chemical-waste containers, waiting to be transported to main base for disposal. I've called the numbers into the National Emergency Materials Center, but I need you to take a look and see what you think."

Maggie knew the twenty-four-hour hotline should respond within minutes. But even those few minutes could be too late for the people facing the danger of a secondary explosion. She pulled out her own copy of the materials directory and frantically scanned the listed agents that contained the numbers the chief cited. All were flammable, but should burn steadily, not explode. The men around her sagged with relief at the news. The call from the center confirmed her numbers a few minutes later.

"Thank God," the chief muttered. He picked up his hand radio and barked a series of short orders.

"The fire crews have contained most of the fires," the on-scene commander told his assembled team less than fifteen minutes later. "I'm moving the command post forward. Get your stuff. Public Affairs, you need to leave someone here to handle reporters. I don't want them on-scene until we ID the injured. Call me if anyone gets too persistent about wanting to film the scene. I want to clear it before you bring anyone forward. The rest of you gather your gear and move up."

Maggie, with Jack crammed between her and the chaplain, maneuvered her van over the bumpy road leading to the test-control facility. Several ambulances passed in the opposite direction, moving back toward the main road with lights flashing and sirens wailing. As soon as Maggie's van reached the site, the chaplain jumped out to hurry to the small triage area set up.

Maggie and Jack stood back to observe the devastated control facility and its surrounding area. Flames had scorched the earth all around and peeled the paint from the main metal building and its adjacent utility sheds. Electrical lines hung loose and snapping on one side of the building. Maggie directed Jack to get on the radio to the architectural section back at the main base. They needed a general idea of the floor plans of the main facility so they could check for underground drains that might carry burning fuel. While Jack was on the radio, Maggie desperately scanned the crowd of hurrying people.

She identified firefighters, security police, disaster-response team members in their distinctively marked hard hats, medics and a couple of frantic-looking civilians huddled to one side of the site. But, try as she might, she couldn't see any figure that came near Mac's dimensions.

She shivered with gut-wrenching fear when the chief approached her, his face grave.

"The doc just confirmed that Colonel MacRae was one of the injured. His burns aren't too bad, but he inhaled a lot of smoke pulling one of the crew out from under some burning debris. They've already transported him to the hospital."

He reached out a hand to steady her as she rocked back on her heels. "I'm sorry—I wish I could tell you more about how he is. But maybe Doc—"

Maggie was racing toward the clump of medics before he could finish.

The doctor assured her that Mac's condition, although critical, was stable. He was unconscious, and they feared lung damage. The doc couldn't, or wouldn't, say more, but he did add that the hospital commander, a noted surgeon, was already with the emergency-room crew awaiting the ambulances. Mac would be in good hands.

Maggie worked frantically with Jack to cover her checklist items. She guessed it would be at least three or four hours until the initial assessment was complete, and then there'd be days and weeks of investigative reports. But Jack could handle it from here.

The on-scene commander took her report, agreed Jack could handle the cleanup, then arranged a ride for her back to the main base in one of the police cars. With a grim shake of his head, he returned to the business at hand.

Chapter Eleven

"Maggie!"

The thin wavering cry greeted her as she got off the elevator and hurried down the pale hospital corridor toward the intensive-care unit. She recognized Davey's voice even before two figures came hurtling toward her from a small waiting room to one side. She knelt down to hug one small body in each arm.

"Don't cry, Danny," she whispered to a dark head buried in her shoulder. "I talked to the doctors downstairs. They're sure your dad will be okay."

Actually, the hospital commander, whom she'd met at a couple of parties, said he was sure Mac would pull through. Something about his being a tough son of a—

"Maggie, they say Colonel Mac has burned his lungs. That he's on a respirator." Mrs. Harris joined the group in the middle of the hallway. Maggie held out her hand and Kate gripped it hard.

Maggie loosened her hold on the twins. "Come on, troops. Let's get out of the hallway before the hospital orderlies sweep us up and out."

When the small group were seated in the waiting area, Kate wadded her handkerchief into a tight ball. "Did you say you talked to the doctors, Maggie?"

"Yes. The hospital commander stopped me on my way up here. He'd just checked on Mac and said he was doing as well as could be expected. I guess that's medical jargon for hanging in there. He's well enough for them to allow me a quick visit, anyway. Have you seen him?" she asked the boys.

"No, they wouldn't let us in," Davey answered waveringly. "The nurses have been real nice, though," he added after a quick swallow. "They come out every so often to let us know how he's doing."

"Well, I got the okay from the big man himself, so I'll go check. I'll see if they'll let you in."

Maggie wiped her finger gently across Danny's cheek to catch a lingering tear. She ached to kiss them both, but wasn't sure just how nine-year-old boys felt about kisses. She contented herself with one last ferocious squeeze.

The nurse in charge led her to one of the six beds that formed an open circle in front of the monitoring desk. Maggie wasn't prepared for the sight of Mac lying so still and helpless. He had a respirator tube taped to his mouth and various intravenous lines running into one arm. Gauzy tentlike structures covered both arms almost to his shoulders. A light gauze pad ran down one side of his face, from forehead to chin.

"Oh, Mac," she whispered. She wanted desperately to hold his hand, touch some part of him, but was afraid to disturb any of the bandages or cause him pain. She looked helplessly at the nurse standing on the other side of the bed.

"Don't worry," the woman said with a sympathetic smile. "He's doing fine. They've already decided not to send him with the others to the burn center in San Antonio. All these tubes make him look a lot worse off than he is."

Maggie smiled her thanks as the older woman turned to leave. She spent the next few minutes in a chair pulled up close to Mac's side, whispering softly to him. She could never recall afterward just what she tried to tell him in those first worry-filled moments.

The boys and Kate waited for her anxiously, along with a gathering crowd of Mac's co-workers and friends. Several officers who knew Mac were there already, some with their wives. The Eglin commander, a major-general almost as big as Mac, arrived within a half hour. He spoke to each of the boys and to Maggie and Kate after he'd taken a quick look in on Mac. The boys were allowed one short visit, which they took surprisingly well, before agreeing to go home with their friend Joey's dad.

Time passed in a blur for Maggie after that. It seemed as if there was a constant stream of folks coming to inquire about Mac. A surprising number knew her and knew of her relationship with him. Finally, late that evening, the traffic died down and it was just Kate and Maggie. They were allowed brief visits on the hour. Throughout the long night, the two women took turns making trips into the intensive-care unit, and their shared worry brought them closer.

Maggie spent her short spells at Mac's bedside perched on the edge of a hard chair, whispering soft nonsense to the accompanying hum of the hospital machinery. She finally worked up the nerve to touch him gently on his sheet-covered thigh. With every light stroke she thought about their last conversation, when he had told her he wanted them to marry. And with every stroke, she knew that was what she wanted, too, more than anything else in the world.

The same pattern repeated itself the next day. Kate convinced Maggie to bring some things to the house and stay with her and the boys, rather than make the long lonely drive around the bay to her Destin condo. She moved into a spare bedroom and managed to keep Woof out long enough for a brief nap in the afternoon before heading back to the hospital.

Mac's father arrived that evening. Maggie would've felt awkward if he hadn't greeted her with a warm twinkle in his blue eyes, which looked so like his son's her breath caught in her throat.

"So this is the little girl Mac's told me about." He grinned. The older man carried his years well on his big frame. "I understand you're soon to become part of the family," he added, taking her hand in both of his.

Maggie nodded slowly, but without hesitation. Another line crossed, she thought. "If he still wants me. I'm afraid I've given your son a rough time."

"Good," his loving dad replied with deep satisfaction. "Nothing worthwhile is ever easy in life."

He spent several hours at the hospital before Maggie convinced him to go home with Kate for the night.

Much later, when the hospital had settled into that peculiar somnolent state during which patients rested and the staff worked quietly, Maggie went in for her hourly visit and found Mac awake. He tried to grin at her around the tube taped to his mouth and failed miserably. It was the most gorgeous grimace Maggie had ever seen.

"Hello, Mac." She smiled down at him. "'Bout time you decided to rejoin the living." She sat down and began what by now was an unconscious light stroking of his thigh. "Kate and the boys and your dad were here earlier. They're all okay," she told him. She knew the boys would be his first concern.

"How...how long?" he managed to get out around the tube.

"Two days now. I'm not sure how much you remember. There was an accident, a cable broke and hit a vehicle."

Mac nodded. He remembered everything. Including the screams of the man trapped under the burning vehicle.

"Three men were hurt. They're still not sure if the one you pulled out will make it. They were all taken to the burn center in San Antonio."

He lifted one singed brow in query and nodded at his arms, still under their light gauzy tents.

"You've got second-degree burns on both arms and on one side of your face. The doctors were afraid you'd seriously damaged your lungs, but it's not as bad as they first thought. They'll give you the details now that you're awake."

She turned to alert the nurse of Mac's consciousness. A swarm of medical specialists soon surrounded him, and Maggie retreated to the waiting room. Alone in the dim light, she huddled in one corner of the couch. She drew up her legs, rested her folded arms on her knees and gave way to the tears she'd held back all those terrifying hours.

When she finally went back in to see Mac, he was asleep again. She looked at the tube taped to his mouth and wished with all her heart it was gone, so that she could hear her mountain rumbling in her ear again.

Chapter Twelve

A week later, Maggie almost wished the tube was back in Mac's mouth. He'd turned out to be a terrible patient, one of those men who were never sick and didn't believe anyone who tried to tell him his body needed time to heal. He responded gruffly to the nurses' orders and was extremely vocal in his opinion of the food they served. He told the doctors not to order any drugs or painkillers after just two days. If his burns pained him, he wouldn't admit it. As Maggie came up for her afternoon visit, she could hear his deep gravelly voice halfway down the hall.

"I don't care what the doctor says—I want up! I refuse to use that blasted bedpan again."

"Colonel, you can't, ah, do anything for yourself with those bandaged hands. This is better for you until—"

"I'll manage, dammit!"

Maggie shook her head at his clenched jaw and angry blue eyes as she strode into the room. Two young nurses turned to her with palpable relief. The ward staff had learned quickly she was the only one who could control their patient. The two nurses gave her a thankful glance and left.

"For heaven's sake, Mac, act your age. You've got to stop terrorizing those lieutenants. They're just trying to do their jobs."

Mac watched her toss down a pile of magazines and stand at the foot of his bed, hands on her hips. The sight of her pile of curls tied up with a blue silk scarf and matching soft silk shirt made his frustration level rise dangerously.

"They can damn well go ply their trade on someone else," he grumbled. "And take their bedpan with them."

"You know you can't do anything for yourself with those bandaged hands," Maggie tried patiently.

"Oh, yeah?" His grumpy look was replaced by a decided leer. "Wanna bet? These bandages are the only things that stand between you and being kissed senseless. I think I can manage at least a demure peck or two, even with them on. Come here."

"No way! The last time I got close, you ended up showing your buns to the general's wife when you tried to wrestle me onto the bed just as she came in. Nice conduct for a senior officer!"

"Maggie, come here."

She eyed him for a long moment, then gave in to the soft command. Better the bed than his trying to chase her around the room.

He sighed as she settled gingerly next to him in the wide hospital bed. "I've been waiting for you all afternoon," he said, nuzzling the golden head beside his on the pillow.

Maggie sighed. She relaxed contentedly and let the scent and feel and warmth that was Mac surround her.

"By the way," he added with seeming casualness, "Dad was here again this morning. He wants to know what we want for a wedding present. Does he know something I don't?"

Maggie looked up into his face in dismay. It was her own fault, she told herself. She should have said something sooner.

She'd been trying to bring up the subject of their future ever since Mac had regained consciousness. She wanted desperately to tell him that all her wanderlust was gone, burned up in the flames that almost took him, as well. To her dismay, she'd discovered that taking a man up on a marriage offer he hadn't renewed was a little tricky. She and Mac had had precious few moments alone since he'd been moved out of intensive care to a private room. It seemed the man knew half the people on the darn base. Someone was always there, even late in the evenings.

Well, it looked like her future father-in-law had made the first move for her. As long as they had a few moments alone now, she might as well follow up.

"Your father seemed to know about your rash offer, or rather, order, of marriage. If the order still stands, Colonel, I want very much to marry you," Maggie told him softly.

"Dammit, woman, you picked a fine time for this!" he roared.

"What?"

Maggie bounced off the bed. She'd have whacked the jerk with his own bedpan for startling her so if she wasn't so confused by his response.

"Hell, woman, I've been aching for you ever since I regained consciousness and found you stroking my thigh. Do you have any idea what that does to a man who's numb everywhere but one particular unburned spot? The nurses are going to have to build another little tent pretty soon to cover the evidence of my frustration."

Dumfounded, Maggie gaped at him.

"And then you have the nerve to bring up marriage when I can't even take you in my arms and kiss you and . . . do all the other things a man should do when the woman he loves says she'll marry him."

"You idiot," Maggie shouted. "First you order me to marry you, now you won't even take yes for an answer when I give it. Well, I've got news for you, Alastair Duggan MacRae—yes, your father filled me in on the Duggan—we're going to be married and that's that. The boys are already planning the ceremony."

Maggie took devilish satisfaction in Mac's surprised look. "They're part of this, too," she went on. "They've got a great idea for a guitarist for the reception. Someone with a safety pin in his ear, I think." She ignored his low groan.

"And Kate is already designing the cake. She's got visions of a pile of sweet gooey frosting five layers high."

This time she grinned at Mac's long moan. She was beginning to enjoy herself.

"Your dad is making reservations for the honeymoon. It's a toss-up between Disney World and fishing in Michigan. The boys are torn, but I think the vote is going to be for Disney World. Kate's never been there, you see."

Maggie's green eyes sparkled in pure mischief. She imagined there wouldn't be many times she'd have her mountain lying helpless. She enjoyed the rare sensation of having the upper hand.

Mac gave her a long-suffering look.

"And if you don't behave yourself and follow the doctor's orders we may line up Woof to stand in for the groom. He's about the same size, but has a much better disposition."

The corners of Mac's mouth turned up in his slow, lazy, incredibly sexy smile. Maggie thought she might drown in the flow of emotion that washed over her. Lord, she loved that smile. Not to mention the hunk of male that went with it.

"Well, you may think you have all the details covered. But I've got news for you, too. *I'm* going to pick out the wedding dress."

And he did. It was a loose, baggy creation with yards of netting that somehow managed to hang on Maggie's every curve.

LOOK TO THE PAST FOR FUTURE FUN AND EXCITEMENT!

The past the Harlequin Historical way, that is. 1994 is going to be a banner year for us, so here's a preview of what to expect:

* The continuation of our bigger book program, with titles such as *Across Time* by Nina Beaumont, *Defy the Eagle* by Lynn Bartlett and *Unicorn Bride* by Claire Delacroix.

* A 1994 March Madness promotion featuring four titles by promising new authors Gayle Wilson, Cheryl St. John, Madris Dupree and Emily French.

* Brand-new in-line series: DESTINY'S WOMEN by Merline Lovelace and HIGHLANDER by Ruth Langan; and new chapters in old favorites, such as the SPARHAWK saga by Miranda Jarrett and the WARRIOR series by Margaret Moore.

* *Promised Brides*, an exciting brand-new anthology with stories by Mary Jo Putney, Kristin James and Julie Tetel.

* Our perennial favorite, the Christmas anthology, this year featuring Patricia Gardner Evans, Kathleen Eagle, Elaine Barbieri and Margaret Moore.

Watch for these programs and titles wherever Harlequin Historicals are sold.

HARLEQUIN HISTORICALS...
A TOUCH OF MAGIC!

HHPROMO94

STOLEN
moments
TM